Alex stared █████ ████ █████████ ████████ g blurted out, "██████ ████ ██████████ ████████ at us. You got ████ █████ █████ ████████ ██ even going to mention that?"

Holt frowned. "I wasn't planning on it. At least not until I have an idea on the matter."

Alex shook her head. "Well, at least let me dress that wound while you try to formulate a good idea about someone trying to kill us. And make sure you change the dressing twice a day. The last thing you want is an infection."

"Good advice," he said and stepped closer to her, knowing what he was about to do was a really bad idea, but unable to come up with one good reason not to.

He pulled her close to him in one sudden motion that made her gasp. Before he could change his mind, he lowered his lips to hers.

Immediately she pushed back and stared at him, her eyes wide. "I think I'll wait in the truck."

"It's not safe out there," he said.

"It's safer than being in here."

JANA DeLEON

THE RECKONING

HARLEQUIN®

entertain, enrich, inspire™

To my friend Leslie Langtry.
Together, we will remain sane with our focus on that private island, cabana boys and the invention of calorie-free beer.

ISBN-13: 978-0-373-74701-6

Recycling programs
for this product may
not exist in your area.

THE RECKONING

ABOUT THE AUTHOR

Jana DeLeon grew up among the bayous and small towns of southwest Louisiana. She's never actually found a dead body or seen a ghost, but she's still hoping. Jana started writing in 2001 and focuses on murderous plots set deep in the Louisiana bayous. By day, she writes very boring technical manuals for a software company in Dallas. Visit Jana at her website, www.janadeleon.com.

Books by Jana DeLeon

CAST OF CHARACTERS

Alexandria Bastin—The sexy psychiatrist was the only person who believed her cousin when she insisted her six-year-old daughter had been kidnapped and not taken by her estranged husband. But finding the missing child means that Alex comes face-to-face with her own ghosts in the form of temporary sheriff Holt Chamberlain.

Holt Chamberlain—He'd hoped leaving Vodoun would eliminate his desire for Alex, but ten years of military service hadn't lessened it one bit. Now a child is missing and his only chance of finding her is working side by side with Alex, the woman he ran away from all those years ago.

Sarah Rhonaldo—Her opinions of her estranged husband were at an all-time low, but Sarah didn't think for one minute that Bobby had kidnapped his daughter. She is convinced a stranger has taken Erika and is afraid it had something to do with her own childhood secrets.

Bobby Rhonaldo—Sarah's cheating husband has his share of faults, but he's always been a good father. Would he really take Erika away from the mother she loves more than anything?

Erika Rhonaldo—Has the six-year-old's father taken her to South America or was she lured into the swamp by the witch that lives on the island?

Sheriff Jasper Conroy—Holt's cousin has always despised Sarah for reasons Holt has never been able to uncover, but would his cousin's hatred for the woman really descend to refusing to help her find her missing child?

Lorraine Conroy—Sheriff Conroy's mother knows the real reason behind her son's hatred for Sarah, but that is one of many secrets she's determined to take to the grave.

Martin Rommel—Lorraine's much younger friend is the cause of raised eyebrows everywhere in Vodoun, but is he using the older woman for her money or does he have other reasons for sticking close to the Conroy family?

Mathilde Tregre—Fifteen years ago she was accused of kidnapping little girls and sacrificing them on her island in order to gain mystical power, but the police never found any evidence to convict her.

Prologue

New Orleans Press, October 31, 1976

Three children are missing in Mystere Parish from the tiny bayou town of Vodoun. All three attended first grade at Vodoun Elementary and had been playing in the backyard of one girl's home before the mother realized they were gone. A search party of the neighboring swamp has yielded only a hair ribbon and a torn piece from one girl's dress.

According to the sheriff's department, the investigation is ongoing, and they are looking into several possibilities. Locals have formed their own search parties to continue sweeping the swamp, and some of them have a different take. Some believe that a voodoo priestess who lives on an island in the swamp kidnapped the girls for sacrifice. The island, which is surrounded by thousands of toy dolls in various states of decay, is the sort of things nightmares are made of.

The sheriff's department states that deputies have searched the island and are satisfied that the girls were never there, but this is hardly the first unusual story to emerge from the swamps of Mystere Parish. If anyone has information as to the whereabouts of the missing girls, please contact the Sheriff's department in Vodoun, Louisiana.

—Staff Reporter

Chapter One

Psychiatrist Alexandria Bastin clutched the cell phone at her cousin's words. "Repeat that." She couldn't possibly have heard her correctly.

"The witch took her! She took my baby!" Sarah's wailing pierced Alex's ear, even through the phone.

"Calm down, Sarah," Alex said and waved off a nurse who had paused during her rotation to see if Alex needed help. "Take a deep breath and tell me everything." She hurried down the hall and into her office to escape the normal noises of the busy hospital. "How long has Erika been missing?"

"Since this afternoon. She went down the street to play with her friend." The hysterical tone in Sarah's voice continued to rise with each sentence. "She was supposed to be home at three, but she never came. I waited and waited and she never came."

"What did the friend's mother say?"

"That Erika left in time to get home. She's gone, Alex, and no one will believe me. My baby! What happened to my baby?" Sarah began sobbing. "I called and called but you never answered."

Alex grabbed her purse from her desk drawer and locked her office. "I'm on my way. Sarah, can you hear me?"

The sound of frantic sobbing was all Alex heard as she rushed into the elevator. As soon as the elevator door closed, the call dropped. Alex looked at her display and cursed when she saw the list of missed calls from her cousin. She'd been tied up all afternoon giving a video-taped statement for a commitment hearing and had turned off her phone, but now she wished she hadn't.

Mentally, she willed the elevator to move faster and as soon as the door opened to the parking garage, she ran to her car, pressing in Sarah's number as she ran. The busy signal had her cursing again.

She jumped into her car and tore out of the parking lot toward the highway. Even with a fast car and a lead foot, it would take her at least an hour to get to Sarah's house. She pressed re-dial, and the busy signal sounded once again. Glancing in her rearview mirror, she merged onto the highway and immediately moved to the fast lane.

Out of options, she dialed 9-1-1.

"This is Dr. Alexandria Bastin. I'm a resident psychiatrist at Memorial Hospital in New Orleans. I have reason to believe that a patient is suffering from a serious mental episode and I cannot get her to answer the phone. I'm on my way, but I need someone to check on Sarah Rhonaldo at 152 Cypress Lane in Vodoun."

She pressed her foot down harder on the accelerator and prayed that Sarah hadn't done something foolish. Her cousin had separated from Erika's father three months before, and it hadn't been pleasant—especially not for Sarah's husband, her best friend, or the bed she'd caught them having sex in, as it had met a tragic end, hatchet style.

Alex had managed, with the help of a great attorney, to get the charges reduced to destruction of private property, but Sarah's Paul Bunyan routine hadn't scored her any points with the local sheriff. Given that their families had been warring since the dawn of time, the bed-hatchet escapade cemented Sheriff Conroy's belief that Sarah was worthless trash.

She could only hope Sarah hadn't done anything to jeopardize her health…or her parole. Alex didn't even want to think about what might have happened to Erika until she got face-to-face with Sarah and heard the entire story.

A TRUCK DISPLAYING THE sheriff's logo on the side was in front of Sarah's house when Alex pulled up just before seven p.m. *This can't be good.* She pulled in behind the truck and parked. She'd been hoping for an ambulance, but there was no sign of a paramedic anywhere. Which meant whatever had happened to Sarah, her health was fine, but given that the sheriff was still there, her freedom might be in question.

She grabbed her purse and hurried into the house without bothering to knock. "Sarah," she called, scanning the rooms as she rushed down the hall.

"Back here," Sarah answered, her voice weak.

Alex ran the rest of the way down the hall and into the kitchen and ran straight into the last person in the world she expected or wanted to see.

His shoulders were wider, his upper body harder and leaner than she'd ever seen him. And she'd seen every inch. "Holt," she said, trying to keep her voice steady. "I didn't know you were back."

Ten years ago, he'd run away to war—the

one place he could be certain his past couldn't follow him.

His hands were still on her shoulders, and he stood so close she could feel the heat coming off his body. The smell of his aftershave tickled her nose, and instantly she remembered the last time his hands had been on her body. The last time she'd been completely absorbed with Holt—mind, body and soul.

"Been back for a month now," he said, and looked down at her with those sexy green eyes that had been the cause of many a weak moment on her part.

But no more.

She stepped back so that he was forced to drop his hands, and that was when she noticed the badge on his belt. "You're working for your uncle?"

"I'm just filling in until I figure out what I want to do next and until his broken leg heals."

"Is Sarah okay?"

Holt moved to the side and motioned her into the breakfast nook where Sarah sat, staring out the back window. "You tell me."

Alex walked over to the table and slid onto the chair next to Sarah. Her cousin took one look at her, flung her arms around her neck and began sobbing. "They don't believe me. My baby's gone and they don't believe me."

The volume of her voice increased with every word until she was shouting.

Alex untangled Sarah's arms from her neck and studied her cousin. Her skin was pale, but normal, given the situation. Her eyes were red from crying, but Alex didn't see any disconnect from reality in them.

"Who doesn't believe you?"

Sarah pointed to Holt. "The sheriff's department. They think I'm crazy."

A flash of anger washed over Alex like a tidal wave and she turned to face Holt. "A six-year-old is missing from her own neighborhood in broad daylight. Exactly what does it take for the sheriff's department to become concerned?"

"My uncle said—"

"Your uncle wouldn't have a nice thing to say about Sarah even if it meant avoiding eternal damnation." Alex turned her attention back to Sarah. "I need you to take a deep breath and tell me what happened."

Sarah nodded and took a deep breath, blowing it slowly out. "Right after lunch, Erika went to her friend's house up the street to play. I stood outside and watched her until she went inside their house. She was supposed to be home by three."

"But she didn't come home?"

"No. At three-fifteen, I called her friend's mother to remind Erika to leave, but the mother said Erika had left at five 'til, just like she was supposed to."

"Did the friend's mother watch her walk home?"

"No. Erika walked with her friend all the way to the house and then her friend crossed the street to go to her music lesson."

"Did her friend see Erika go in the house?"

Sarah shook her head. "She said when she was closing the door, she saw Erika checking the mail. But when I came outside to look for her, the mail was lying in the street." Sarah began to cry again. "They think Bobby took her. He's a lying, worthless, cheating waste-of-a-husband, but he's a good father. Bobby would never take Erika away from me."

Alex blew out a breath, trying to make sense of everything Sarah had said. Her cousin's story didn't fill in all the gaps and she had a feeling those gaps were important. Unfortunately, the one person who could give her the answers she needed was the last person she wanted to talk to.

She opened her purse and took out a prescription for antianxiety medication that she'd filled for Sarah the day before. Ever since Sarah's split from Bobby, she'd had trouble sleeping and concentrating. The meds took the edge off and allowed her to act normal even though she didn't feel normal. "I want you to take this," she said, and placed a pill in Sarah's hand. "I need to know everything you can think of. In order to be helpful, you need to be refreshed and calm. While the medicine is doing its job, I want you to take a hot shower."

Sarah opened her mouth to protest, but Alex held up a hand to stop her. "I'm saying this as your doctor. No arguments."

Sarah looked at Alex, her expression wavering between wanting to comply and wanting to argue, then she glanced over at Holt and sighed. "Fine."

Alex rose from the table and pushed a glass of water closer to Sarah. Sarah placed the pill in her mouth and took a big drink, her hand shaking a bit as she lowered the glass back to the table. Her cousin rose from the table and hugged Alex.

"I feel better already because you're here," Sarah said. "You're the smartest person I know. You'll find Erika." Sarah broke off the hug and trudged down the hall toward her bedroom.

Alex stared after her, trying to keep her own heart from breaking over the situation. She and Sarah had been born only a month apart and were more like sisters than cousins. She and

Erika were the only family Alex had left since her own parents had died in a car wreck twelve years before. The day Erika was born, Alex had been almost as proud as Sarah, and to think of that little girl, taken from her home, was beyond upsetting. But one of them had to remain calm and collected, and that role almost always fell to Alex.

She looked over at Holt, who was leaning against the kitchen counter. "I need you to tell me exactly what is going on. No speculation or your uncle's gossip. Cold, hard facts are all I'm interested in."

Holt smiled. "*Cold* was never in your vocabulary when I knew you. *Hard*…well, that's a whole other story."

Alex felt a flush rise up her neck. "And one that will not be remembered or relived now or at any other time. A little girl is missing. Her mother is frantic. Surely, you can tell me something."

Holt's expression changed from teasing to serious.

"Sarah called the sheriff's office this afternoon in a panic. I came out here to see what was up, then followed up on the leads. What she told you is correct. I talked to the friend's mother and she verified the story. I checked with the other neighbors, but no one saw Erika."

"Then why haven't you formed a search party? Do I have to remind you that not a hundred yards from the backyard of this house is the swamp?"

"It rained the past couple of days. I walked a two-mile stretch of the tree line and never saw a single footprint. So unless Erika walked beyond that before entering the swamp, that's not where she is."

Alex nodded, not wanting to admit that so far, everything Holt said made sense. "And this theory about Bobby taking Erika?"

"Pretty much everyone knows about the split between Bobby and Sarah and what caused it, so the sheriff thought I better check with Bobby before sending out an alert and panicking the town." He looked down the hallway for a second then back at Alex. "Is she all right…mentally, I mean?"

"She was angry over Bobby's cheating, and rightly so, and she's clearly upset now and perhaps in a bit of shock. But given the circumstances, I don't see anything wrong with her reactions."

"So she's sane?"

Alex bristled. "I can't discuss a client's medical condition with you. I've already said more than I should have."

"So even if there was something wrong, you wouldn't tell me?"

"*Couldn't* tell you. There's a big difference. But as nothing is wrong, aside from the obvious, this is a pointless discussion. What happened when you talked to Bobby?"

"Nothing. His fourplex unit was stripped clean and so were his bank accounts."

Alex stared, completely taken aback with what Holt had said. "His employer?"

"He gave notice two weeks ago and had already worked his last day. Said he'd gotten a better job in New Orleans."

"And that…that woman?"

Holt grimaced. "Oh, she had plenty to say about Bobby, especially as the affair ended her marriage, too. Apparently, middle-aged, unemployed, uneducated women who sleep with their best friend's husbands aren't exactly desired by employers or anyone else."

"My heart bleeds for her. So did she know where Bobby moved?"

"Yeah, see, that's where it gets interesting. She says he was going back home to Brazil."

Alex froze. "Permanently?"

Holt shrugged. "The New Orleans police haven't turned up a new residence or employer so far."

"You think he stole his child and fled to Brazil? Erika didn't even have a passport."

"Yes, she did. He filed for one a couple months ago."

Alex took a couple of seconds to digest that. "Did Sarah know?"

"Yeah. She said he was planning to take Erika to visit his family in Brazil during summer vacation."

"Sarah knows how to contact his relatives. What do they say?"

"Naturally, they all claim ignorance on the subject."

Alex's mind swam with all the implications of Holt's theory, but no matter how much sense it made on the surface, it didn't add up for Alex, either. "You've checked the airports."

"Of course, and if we'd found anything, this would already be over."

"So that means he didn't take her out of the country."

"No. It just means he didn't fly. Given that he took all his belongings, it's more logical that he's driving."

"So you're going to do nothing?"

"I've notified Louisiana and Texas law enforcement that Erika was missing and sent them photos of her and Bobby and all the information on Bobby's car. I contacted several news agencies here and in Texas, and they've agreed to show a picture and ask viewers to call a hotline if they've seen either of them." Holt sighed. "What else would you like me to do?"

"Nothing," Alex said. "You're right. There's nothing left to do but wait and pray."

Holt nodded. "Then I'll get going and let you take care of Sarah. If you need anything, call dispatch, and they'll get in touch with me."

Alex followed him down the hall to the front door. He stepped outside, then turned back to face her. "I'm really sorry about all of this," he said. "I know my uncle and Sarah have their issues, but I promise you my uncle's beliefs do not interfere with my investigation. I'm doing everything I can to find Erika."

Alex nodded and he turned and walked to his truck. She watched as he drove down the block in the vanishing sunlight. She didn't doubt Holt was doing everything he could. He wasn't the kind of man who took failure lightly—she knew that better than anyone. But Holt didn't know what she did—that Sarah was telling the truth.

There was no way Bobby would have taken Erika away from Sarah. She was as certain of that as she was of anything. And since it was unlikely Erika had gotten lost in the swamp,

Alex knew something very bad had happened to the child.

It was up to her to find out what.

Chapter Two

Holt Chamberlain pulled away from Sarah's house, a million thoughts running through his head. All but one had to do with Alexandria Bastin. He'd known Alex was on her way to Vodoun when he went to Sarah's house, and he thought he'd mentally prepared himself for seeing her again. Now that he had, he realized how egotistical he'd been to think he was prepared.

Like holding up a trash can lid to stave off a tidal wave.

Ten years hadn't taken a single thing away from her. Her face was more mature than the college girl he'd left behind, but still as beautiful as he remembered. Her thick blond hair, a gift from her German mother, had been pulled up on top of her head, but he had no doubt that when released, it would fall in thick waves down her shoulders. And even in her official hospital business suit, he could see her body wasn't missing a trick. She was walking sexy and still as sharp as they came.

He'd been prepared for his body to react, for his heart to tug a bit when he laid eyes on his first love. But what he'd experienced was a total annihilation of senses. There was no preparation for that, short of death.

All that running and he'd landed back in Vodoun right smack in the middle of the same turmoil he'd been in when he'd made the decision to leave. Time and distance hadn't changed anything except allowing him to temporarily forget.

And all of that took a backseat to the one thing that had nothing to do with his past with Alex—Sarah's missing daughter. He couldn't argue with the logic. Everything he'd found backed up his uncle's idea that Bobby had kidnapped his daughter and fled to Brazil, but something didn't feel right to Holt.

Things in Mystere Parish never did.

Something about the stretch of dense swamp that comprised most of the parish was unlike anywhere he'd ever been before, and he'd seen plenty of conflicted places during his military service. Not that Mystere was conflicted. In fact, it appeared to be comprised of small, peaceful towns filled with down-to-earth, law-abiding people. But under that surface of pleasant normalcy, Mystere hid secrets. Some of those secrets eventually rose to the surface.

It was the ones that hadn't yet that concerned Holt.

Hoping his uncle was right for a change, Holt decided to take another look at Bobby and directed his truck toward the fourplex where Bobby had lived. Bobby taking Erica was the simple answer—the good answer. Holt didn't want to think about the options until he'd eliminated the most obvious and the safest for the child.

The deputy had taken statements from the people occupying the two front units this afternoon, but the woman who lived directly across from Bobby in the other rear unit hadn't been home. Maybe she was available now and could fill in some of the gaps.

He was about to pull up in back of the fourplex when his cell phone rang. He checked the display and frowned. His uncle.

Holt's grandfather had married Lorraine after the death of his first wife, Holt's paternal grandmother. After several miscarriages, Jasper Conroy had been a surprise baby for Lorraine. He was only two years older than Holt, but he wore the "Uncle" title as proudly as he did his sheriff's badge. The man's body might be restricted to bed rest, but it hadn't stopped his mouth from traveling far and often.

"Uncle Conroy, what can I do for you?"

"Why aren't you back at the sheriff's office?"

"I've been looking into the Rhonaldo case."

"There is no Rhonaldo case. Bobby Rhonaldo took that kid from that screaming shrew of a wife and skipped the country. Since we don't have the time, the manpower or the jurisdiction to chase him to South America, I expect you to be back in the office in ten minutes."

"To do what, exactly?"

"Whatever I say you need to do. Don't get belligerent with me, boy. I'm still in charge."

Holt struggled to control his tongue. His mother had asked this favor of him so that Jasper could continue to draw his salary and not worry about someone poaching his job. Holt figured it was a heck of a lot of aggravation to take for a favor, but he supposed it was a nice thing to do.

Thanks to the business acumen of his late and mostly absentee father, Holt had enough money to last a lifetime, so working for free didn't bother him at all. But a little consideration wouldn't be out of line, since Jasper was the only one benefiting from Holt's time.

"I figured I needed to be thorough on this one, given your history with Sarah," Holt said.

"I wouldn't want anyone to find a gap in my investigation and use that against you in the next election. If this ends badly, the last thing you need is people saying that if you'd done your job, you could have prevented the death of a six-year-old girl."

There was dead silence for several seconds and Holt knew his uncle recognized the legitimacy of his words and at the same time was mentally cursing nine ways to Sunday that he had to spend even a moment of time on Sarah Rhonaldo. His mother's complete and utter disdain for Sarah went far deeper than a long-standing family feud, but Holt had never been able to determine the real cause of the animosity. It was the best-kept secret in Vodoun.

For that matter, it was probably the only secret in Vodoun.

"Fine, then," Jasper said finally. "Get it over with as fast as possible and put everything you find in the file."

"And if I find anything that indicates something could have happened to Erika besides Bobby taking her?"

"That's not going to happen."

The sound of Jasper slamming the phone down echoed in his ear as he parked. The blinds were open on the unit across from Bobby's and he could see someone moving around inside.

He climbed out of the truck and made his way up the sidewalk, pleased that the neighbor was home and he could finalize this angle of questioning.

The woman who opened the door was young, probably midtwenties, wearing workout clothes and didn't look overly happy that he'd interrupted her routine. He flashed his badge, and her demeanor immediately shifted as she waved him inside.

"Has something happened to my family?" the woman asked, clearly nervous. "Just tell me and get it over with."

Holt realized his faux pas and moved to correct it. "I'm sorry to frighten you, Miss, but I'm here to ask you some questions about your neighbor, Bobby Rhonaldo."

Her shoulders relaxed and she blew out a breath. "Thank God. My parents insisted on retiring in an RV and gallivanting across the country. I remain in a constant state of worry."

"Understandable."

She pulled a bottle of water out of the refrigerator and offered it to him. He shook his head so she twisted the top off the bottle and slid onto a stool at the kitchen counter. "You said you're here about Bobby?"

"Yes. Did you know him?"

"Not well. I'm a nurse at the clinic and I usually work the night shift, so I'm not awake during normal hours. I introduced myself when he moved in, and I've said hello a couple of times when I was coming home from shift and he was leaving for work. That's about it."

Holt nodded. "Were you at home when he moved?"

She frowned. "Yeah. That was weird. My shift started at midnight and when I walked out, two guys were loading Bobby's bed and clothes in a moving truck. I asked about Bobby, but they said he was busy and they'd been paid to move his stuff. They had a key, so I went on to work."

"You said it was weird, though. Why?"

She flipped the cap over between her fingers for a couple of seconds, then blew out a breath. "This is going to sound stupid, but something didn't feel right. I mean, they had a key, and I guess if midnight is when you have time to do something, then that's when you do it. But they…unnerved me, I guess is the best way to put it.

"Look," she continued, "I'm no wilting daisy. I've been living on my own since I was seventeen. Worked my way through college as a nurse's assistant on the nightshift at a hospital in New Orleans. I've seen plenty that would scare the life out of normal people, so for something to bother me is weird."

"Would you recognize them if you saw them again?"

"I think so."

"Thanks," Holt said and handed the woman a card. "If you think of anything else or happen to see the men anywhere, call dispatch and tell them to get in touch with me immediately."

The woman placed the card on the counter and walked him to the door. "Hey," she said, as he was about to walk away. "One of the guys had a tattoo on the back of his right hand."

He stiffened. "Could you tell what it was?"

"It was kinda dark on the sidewalk, but it looked like an eye."

Holt nodded and walked to his truck, hoping his concern at the woman's description hadn't shown on his face. He didn't think the woman was in any danger and didn't want her to worry. But Holt had seen that tattoo before.

On the man who'd murdered his father.

Chapter Three

Alex poured herself a cup of coffee and carried it and decaffeinated tea for Sarah over to the breakfast nook table. The drugs had kicked in, so Sarah appeared less hysterical and more focused than she had been earlier, which was a relief to Alex. She needed Sarah's mind sharp if they were going to find Erika, especially as the police were tapped out on avenues of investigation.

"How are you feeling?" Alex asked, studying her cousin's face. Some of the color had returned, eliminating the ghostlike look she'd worn earlier. The skin around her eyes was puffy and red from crying, but that was hardly unexpected.

"I'm as good as I'm getting for now."

"Do you want anything to eat?"

"No. My stomach couldn't handle it."

"Okay, but don't go too long without having something...even dry toast."

Sarah looked up and gave her a small smile. "Yes, mom."

Alex slid into the chair across from Sarah and pulled a small pad of paper out of her purse to take notes, then changed her mind and reached for her recorder. "Do you mind if I tape this? I want to make sure I get everything."

"That's fine," Sarah said and looked at her, a guilty expression on her face. "I'm sorry for not telling you Holt was back in town."

"I was bound to hear about it sooner or later," Alex said, trying to sound as casual as possible.

"I guess. I'd hoped that he'd figure out what he was doing next and be gone before you crossed paths."

"Well, it's happened and no one shouted or cried. It's been ten years, and we've both moved on with our lives, but I appreciate your concern."

"We're cousins. Looking out for each other is what we do, right?"

Alex reached across the small table and squeezed Sarah's hand. "Absolutely. Have you told your mother?"

"No. She's not…good. Not since Dad died."

"I'll call the nurse's aide tomorrow and talk to her about your mom's care. Let's keep this between us for now." Sarah's mother had been in a nursing home for several years battling lung cancer, but ever since the death of her husband she'd seemed to give up entirely.

"Are you ready to talk?"

Sarah nodded and Alex slipped a blank tape into the recorder and turned it on. "Start with what you told me earlier, so I can get it on tape, okay?"

Her cousin recounted the details she'd provided earlier with Alex interrupting to clarify names and times. When she was done, Alex said, "When you called me, you said the witch took Erika. What did you mean?"

Sarah stared blankly over Alex's shoulder and out the window. "You know what I meant."

Alex felt a trickle of fear run up her spine. "That stuff about the witch was all a story. You know…something parents made up to keep us kids from playing in the swamp."

"Was it, really?" Sarah locked her gaze on Alex. "Do you know that for certain? You saw the same thing on that island as I did. Are you going to deny that?"

A chill passed over Alex and she crossed her arms and leaned on the table. "I'm not denying what we saw, nor that it scared the life out of me. But the police never found any proof that the woman who lived there took those kids."

"The *witch* that lived there," Sarah corrected. "The police didn't want to believe."

"Believe what?" Alex blew out a breath. "That a witch on an island in a swamp kidnapped children and used them as sacrifices in a voodoo ritual? Of course, they didn't want to believe something like that, but it wouldn't stop them from investigating. There was never any evidence that those kids had been on the island."

"The evidence was burned in the ceremony. You know something about the old ways, Alex, even if your current life has you locked into science. You know the swamps of Mystere Parish are full of people who practice black arts and have for hundreds of years."

Alex threw up her hands. "Even if it were all true, what makes you think Erika is on the island?"

"Because." Sarah rose from the table and walked into the kitchen. She climbed onto a step stool to open a cabinet above the refrigerator and pulled out something in a brown paper bag. "I found this in her room, hidden under her bed."

She opened the bag and pulled out a doll with blond hair and blue eyes and placed it on the table. The blood rushed to Alex's head and she gripped the edge of the table to steady herself as a wave of dizziness washed over her.

It couldn't be. Not after all this time.

"Where did she get this?" she asked, struggling to maintain a calm tone.

"Not in any store, that's for sure. I looked it up online. That doll hasn't been manufactured in over thirty years."

"Did you ask her?"

"Of course I asked. After I had a heart attack and then managed to regain control. She said she found it in the backyard at the edge of the swamp, but she was lying."

Alex stared. "How do you know?"

Sarah shrugged. "She's my kid. I know when she's lying. I pushed the issue, but she stuck to her story."

"Have you told her about…I mean warned her in a way she could understand?"

"I told her an old, evil woman lived in the swamp and that it wasn't safe for little girls to go into the swamp without an adult. She's always stayed away before. I checked all her shoes and her rubber boots, but there was no sign she'd been in the swamp or tried to wash away the evidence."

Alex's mind raced, trying to absorb everything Sarah said…trying to make sense of all of it. "When did you find the doll?"

"Three days ago." Sarah slumped back into her chair. "And then there was the crow."

"What crow?"

"It was on the clothesline outside Erika's bedroom window every morning for the last week when I went in to wake her. I closed the blinds and went outside to shoo it away, but every morning, it was right back in place."

Sarah shivered. "Last night, I heard a noise out back. I looked out the kitchen window and could make out the outline of the crow just sitting there. Like it was watching her, even though the blinds were closed." She looked straight at Alex. "You know it's an omen."

"No." Alex shook her head. "I don't know any such thing."

"What about those birds that fell from the sky last week? It was all over the news. Hundreds of them, Alex, lying everywhere in Mystere Parish."

"There are theories—"

Sarah waved a hand, cutting her off. "I know all about the theories, and I know what Sam LeBlanc down at Animal Control told me— that the vet couldn't find anything wrong with any of the birds he autopsied. They're lying so they don't cause a panic."

"They just haven't figured out the reason, yet," Alex said, forbidding her mind to wander into Sarah's realm of thinking.

"We have to go out there," Sarah whispered.

"No!"

"Why not?" Sarah challenged. "If there's really no danger, as you suggest, then what's the harm?"

"Because the swamp contains all sorts of dangers that aren't mystical. You know that as well as anyone. Don't play stupid now. I won't listen to it."

"So you think an alligator or two should keep me from looking for my baby?"

Alex took one look at the determined look on Sarah's face and knew she'd never win this argument. "You can't just go tromping around the swamp without a plan. Neither one of us owns a boat, and we haven't fired a weapon since we were kids. We're not equipped for this."

"So we rent a boat, and I know plenty of people who'd loan us rifles. It's not like you forget how to use one altogether, you know."

"No. We went to that island twenty years ago. I don't even know if we could find it, and even if we did, we could be arrested for being there." A thought flashed through her mind and as hard as she tried to shut it down, it was the only thing that made sense.

"What?" Sarah asked. "You have that look like you thought of something. I'm desperate. I'll do anything to get my baby back."

Alex nodded, her mind made up. "We don't

have the authority or the equipment to get to the island, but I know someone who does."

"Holt?" Sarah shook her head. "His uncle will never let him do that...not for me."

Alex clicked off the recorder and stuffed it in her purse along with her notebook. "So I'll ask him to do it for me."

Sarah bit her lower lip, but a tiny bit of hope flickered in her eyes. "What if he says no?"

"He won't say no." Alex rose from the table and bent over to kiss Sarah's cheek. "He owes me."

HOLT WAS JUST CLOSING UP his office at the sheriff's department when Alex strode in the front door. He took one look at the determined look on her face and knew he was in for it. He'd seen that look many times before, and it always ended with Alex getting her way or getting angry. Given the situation between Sarah and his uncle, he didn't see how this was going to end well for him at all.

"I need to speak to you," she said, her voice clipped and professional. She glanced over at the dispatcher, then back at him. "Alone."

He opened the office door and waved her inside. "Did you learn anything more from Sarah?"

"Yes, but you're not going to like it." She recounted Sarah's story about the doll and the crow.

Holt leaned back in his chair, trying to ignore the overwhelming feeling that he was on shaky ground. Sarah's fears were outrageous, but what didn't compute was why Alex had brought them to him.

"You can't possibly think that a six-year-old managed to find that island, steal a doll and get back home without her mother noticing she was missing."

"No, but I also don't think she ordered a thirty-year-old doll off eBay and paid for it with animal crackers, either. What if someone left the doll for her to find? What if someone gave it to her? All I know is what Sarah told me. Everything started happening after Erika brought the doll into the house."

"You know I don't believe in that stuff," he said finally, but even then, that niggle of doubt had already started in the back of his mind. "Maybe when we were kids it seemed plausible, but I thought we'd grown up."

"We have, and normally, I would try to diminish or redirect someone's thoughts away from this line of thinking, but Sarah's child is missing. No amount of logic or scientific explanation or even calling her childish is going to talk her out of this. Either you lock Sarah up to keep her out of the swamp, or someone is going to have to check that island for Erika."

"Someone?" He stared at her for a moment, then shook his head. "Oh, no. I'm not going out there."

"You scared?"

Holt bristled and sat upright in the chair. "Hardly. But that island is private property and I have no grounds for a warrant and even less for trespassing."

"It's not trespassing if you go to ask questions, is it? You don't even know if the woman is still there. She wasn't young when we were kids. Maybe she's dead. Maybe the island is empty. Regardless, you have every right to walk up there and ask anyone you find if they've seen a missing little girl."

Holt searched his mind for an argument, but he couldn't latch onto one. Not a legal one, anyway.

"Of course," Alex continued, "if you're concerned that your uncle won't approve, I could always hire a guide and go myself. I'm sure I can find someone at the docks who's willing to take me out there."

"No! You're not traipsing around that swamp with some underemployed fisherman looking to make a quick buck."

Alex leaned forward in her chair. "You lost

the right to have any input in my life a long time ago. Either you do this with me, or I do it with someone else. Rest assured, I'm going into that swamp to look for Erika, if for no other reason than to put Sarah's mind at ease."

Holt held in a string of cuss words that would only hack Alex off and wouldn't make him feel any better about the situation, anyway. He knew he was fighting a losing battle.

Something had happened to Alex and Sarah many years ago in that swamp—something they refused to tell Holt about, but something that scared them so badly it had changed them permanently. If Sarah thought there was any risk of Erika encountering the same thing they had—whatever that was—he knew nothing short of death or arrest would keep her out of the swamp.

"Fine," he said, "but I'm not going into that swamp at night and neither are you. That's not up for discussion, regardless of what *rights* I lost."

She rose from her chair. "I have no problem with waiting until daylight."

"Six, then. At the dock."

"I'll bring coffee." She gave him a single nod and walked out of the sheriff's office.

I'll bring the questions. If ever Holt was going to get an answer to what had happened in that swamp years ago, it would be now, when it might affect his ability to find Erika. And you could bet he was going to ask.

Through the plate-glass window, Holt watched Alex drive away and for the second time that day felt as if he'd been hit by a truck. Managing an entire day alone with Alex, without wanting her, was going to be impossible. He'd known that as soon as he'd seen her walk into Sarah's house. And he had no idea what excuse he was going to give his uncle for requisitioning the sheriff department's airboat and cruising around the swamp all day.

But he was going to have to think of something.

He didn't think for one minute that a witch on an island in the swamp had taken Erika, but he didn't quite believe Bobby had, either. That left him in a quandary, and Holt didn't like unanswered questions. This situation was full of them.

Reaching into the desk drawer, he pulled out his uncle's whiskey bottle and poured himself a shot. He wasn't about to admit to Alex that Sarah's story had unnerved him just a bit. He'd have liked to blame his upbringing—a superstitious, overprotective mother and an absentee father—but it was more than that. During his time overseas with the military, he'd been special ops, and he'd spent some time in places the military wasn't technically supposed to be.

He'd seen a lot of things he couldn't explain. So many that he stopped dismissing ideas just because they didn't compute in a traditional way, the way he had when he'd been a boy in Vodoun. Maybe Erika had found the doll somewhere she wasn't supposed to be and that was why she lied, but it was far more likely that a stranger had given Erika the doll. Sarah, being a good parent, would have cautioned Erika not to talk to strangers, much less take something from them, which was why the girl would have lied.

None of that explained who had given a thirty-year-old doll to a little girl, where Erika or Bobby were, the mysterious staring crow or the birds falling from the sky. Except coincidence.

And Holt hated coincidence even more than he did unanswered questions.

Chapter Four

Alex pulled up to the dock at five minutes till six, already nervous about the day before it even started. The local weatherman had reported a disturbance in the Gulf of Mexico that was due to hit Vodoun that evening. The sky was already gray and overcast and made everything seem even grimmer.

Holt stood on the dock talking to one of the local fishermen, and Alex couldn't help but notice how good he looked in ragged jeans, a black T-shirt and steel-toe boots. Time certainly hadn't erased his sex appeal, and that frightened her.

But not as much as their destination.

Twenty years ago, Alex had promised herself she'd never set foot in the swamp again, and all these years she'd kept that promise. Erika and Sarah were the only reason she was going there now.

Let's get this over with.

She climbed out of the car and reached back inside for the two coffees in the center console. The fisherman was still talking to Holt, who gave her a nod as she approached. When the fisherman saw her, he wrapped up his conversation and headed to his boat.

"I hope that's strong and black," Holt said.

Alex handed him one of the cups. "Is there another kind?"

"Not in my book." Holt took a sip of the coffee. "You ready?"

She sat her coffee down on the pier. "Yeah. Let me grab my things."

She hurried to her car and pulled her backpack from the passenger's seat. Slinging it over her shoulder, she headed back to the dock.

Holt looked down the bayou, then back at her feet. "This is going to be rough. I'm glad you wore good boots."

"Just because I live in the city doesn't mean I've forgotten what the bayou's like," Alex said.

She placed her backpack on the pier and removed a nine-millimeter from the side pocket. She checked the clip for the third time that morning, then slipped the gun back into the pocket, zipping it tight.

"I don't remember nines when we were kids," Holt commented. "Or is that something you picked up in the big city?"

"Actually, it belongs to Ms. Maude. I paid her a visit last night after I got Sarah to sleep."

"Ms. Maude? The crazy old cat lady on Miller Lane?"

"No. Ms. Maude, who likes cats, whose father was a Precision Military Weapons Specialist and who happens to have a target gallery in her barn."

"That explains a lot," Holt said, "especially about her single status."

"So what you're saying is that Ms. Maude might have married if all the men in Vodoun weren't a bunch of wimps?"

"I think it's safer if I don't say anything else at all." He took another drink of his coffee and glanced down at her mug, which was still sitting on the dock.

She placed her backpack in the boat and scooped up her coffee. "Don't even think about it," she said. "I'd kill people for less."

Holt sighed and untied the airboat from the dock. "I don't know how far I'll make it on one cup of coffee."

Alex stepped into the airboat. "There might be a full thermos in my backpack, but you're going to have to earn it."

Holt pushed the boat from the dock and jumped in with a grin. "Well, why didn't you say so?" He leaned over, preparing to kiss her.

Alex put one hand on his chest to stop him. "Not like that."

"That used to be the way I earned things."

"The price has increased. Inflation, you know?"

He raised one eyebrow. "I guess that's what happens when things age."

Before Alex could retort, he started the engine and climbed into the driver's seat. Alex turned around and looked over the bow of the boat as Holt took off from the dock. She waved at a couple of fishermen as they made their way up the channel from the dock. At the end of the channel, where the fisherman turned left to the open waters of the lake, Holt turned right into the narrow bayous and inlets that led deeper into the swamp.

Holt slowed as they progressed through the tiny channels, the edges of the airboat sometimes scraping the bank on both sides. It was denser than Alex remembered. Moss clung to almost every branch of the cypress trees that created a canopy over the bayou. The deeper into the swamp they went, the more dim the light became until it seemed almost as if twilight had come, even though it wasn't yet seven a.m.

The darkness seemed to set upon her like a wet blanket, weighing her down and making breathing more difficult. She closed her eyes and took a deep breath, blowing it slowly out. She'd known that coming here again would affect her, but she'd underestimated by how much. She'd spent a lot of years in New Orleans concentrating on her education and then her practice. And even more years trying to put the swamps of Mystere Parish out of her mind. Apparently, it had been wasted time. It seemed that for every hundred yards they moved deeper into the swamp, she could feel her heartbeat kick up just a bit.

Alex glanced back at Holt and the grim look on his face didn't help calm her at all. For more reasons than one, he probably regretted agreeing to do this. If he hadn't known how absolutely bull-headed Sarah could be, Alex knew, he wouldn't have agreed at all. But checking it out himself was preferable to forming a search party to look for Sarah, who would walk on hot coals to save her daughter.

Holt cut off the engine and Alex looked back at him. "Is something wrong?"

He pulled a cane pole from the bottom of the boat and began to push the boat down the channel. "We're almost there. I didn't figure I should announce our approach with a turbine, even though the sound has probably carried for miles."

Alex nodded as the smell of mud and rotting foliage hit her. The blanket of decaying water lilies was the only indication of the water beneath, and the brush from the bank met the water's edge, giving the appearance of a solid surface of brown and yellow. The sunlight was almost gone completely, leaving them to push farther into the darkness.

As they rounded a corner, Holt pointed to a dilapidated pier, almost hidden behind cattails and marsh grass. Alex gripped her seat with both hands trying to slow her racing heart.

The dolls.

She thought she'd prepared herself for coming to the island again, but she couldn't have been more wrong. The dolls had always littered the island, attached to every tree branch and post—some of them just resting on the ground. Some said the witch woman placed the dolls there to attract the children she sacrificed. Some said the dolls had been blessed and placed there by the villagers, hoping to imprison the witch in the swamp forever.

Alex didn't know the truth and doubted anyone else did, either. What she did know is that the dolls scared the hell out of her. Sitting, dangling…in various states of rot and decay. Torn dresses and pants. Some missing parts. But all of them with one thing in common—the eyes were intact.

Hundreds of pairs of eyes, watching them as they drew closer to the bank.

Blue eyes, green eyes, brown eyes. Each one following their every movement.

Alex drew in a ragged breath and slowly blew it out. She had to focus. Finding Erika was her only priority. All her fears and thoughts of the past could wait until she was locked safely inside her townhome back in New Orleans.

Without a doll in sight.

Holt guided the boat to the side of the pier until it made contact with the bank. At one time, there had been a path from this pier to the old woman's cabin, but Alex could barely make out a trail now. Clearly, no one passed this way often.

"Are you ready?" Holt asked when the boat rested against the bank.

Alex nodded, unable to trust her voice at the moment. She rose from her seat, lifting her backpack as she went. She walked to the front of the boat, ready to step onto the bank, then stopped cold.

On the lowest branch of a cypress tree directly in front of her sat a blond doll in a blue dress, just like the doll Sarah had found in Erika's room. Just like the doll she'd never wanted to see again. But unlike the doll Erika had, this doll was old and weathered, the blue dress hanging in tatters on the pale body. The blond hair matted and twisted around the doll's body.

And this doll's eyes were closed.

Alex felt her pulse racing in her temples. She took another deep breath and before she could change her mind, stepped onto the bank. The instant her foot made contact with the ground, the doll's eyes flew open.

"Oh!" Alex choked back a cry and stepped back, bumping into Holt who had moved to the front of the boat, just behind her.

Holt caught her by the shoulders, steadying her before she lost her balance in the rocking boat. The doll stared at her, its bright blue eyes seeming to look straight through her and into her soul.

"What's wrong?" Holt asked, his voice low.

"The doll. It opened its eyes when I stepped on the bank."

She looked back at him, certain of the incredulous look she'd find on his face, but instead, he stared intently at the doll.

"It was probably just vibration from your step. When I docked the boat the eyes loosened a bit, and your footstep was the final shake it took for them to open."

His words made complete sense, but Alex

got the impression that even Holt wasn't quite buying his explanation. He just didn't have a better one.

"Let's get this over with," Alex said and stepped onto the bank, deliberately looking past the doll. But as she walked past the cypress tree, she could feel its eyes upon her.

Holt stepped out of the boat, pausing only long enough to pull his pistol from the waistband of his jeans, then stepped in front of her. "Stay close. If you see or hear anything odd, grab the back of my shirt but don't talk. Okay?"

Alex nodded and fell in step behind him as he pushed deeper into the dense undergrowth. The light diminished gradually until it had all but vanished and a thin mist rose from the mossy ground. Despite the cool fall temperature, a sheen of sweat formed quickly on her brow, and she brushed it away with the back of her hand. The humidity was high today because of the approaching storm. Damp leaves from the dense foliage brushed against her bare arms, making her flinch. She pushed spiderwebs out of her way as they passed, but could still feel the remnants tickling her bare skin.

The air seemed thicker, the swamp completely devoid of the noises one would expect to hear. The sound of hers and Holt's footsteps crunching dead marsh grass echoed in the still air. Alex peered around Holt's shoulder, trying to make out a path or structure, but all she saw was more swamp.

All of a sudden, Holt stopped short and she bumped into his back. "What's wrong?" she whispered.

He reached up and moved a sheet of moss from his field of vision and scanned the swamp from left to right. Finally, he shook his head. "I thought I saw something move, but I might have been mistaken."

"There should be something moving out here, right? I mean, should it be this still?"

Holt's grim expression let her know that he'd also noticed the quiet and didn't like it any more than she did. "Maybe it's because of the storm moving in."

"I thought it wasn't going to start until this evening."

"Maybe it's moving faster than the weathermen reported. The marsh creatures know better than humans what's going on with the weather. Likely, it's coming in sooner than they think, which means we need to find the woman and get out of here before the bottom drops out."

Alex nodded, the thought of being stranded on Doll Island in a raging thunderstorm sending her heart fluttering all over again. "Do you have any idea which way to go?"

"It looks like the brush clears a little about twenty yards just south of us. We'll go that way then reassess. I have to tell you, if we don't find a path soon that looks like someone's used it in the last century, I'm not going to venture much farther in this swamp. It would be foolish."

"But Erika—"

"I'm sure Sarah doesn't want or expect you to put yourself in danger, not even for her daughter. We don't do Sarah or Erika any good dead, and there's far more dangerous things in this swamp than a bunch of creepy dolls and an old woman."

"Fine," Alex said, knowing he was right but hating it at the same time. Granted, odds were against their finding any sign of Erika on the island for so many reasons, but if they returned so quickly with nothing, Sarah would be upset.

Holt pushed the brush to the side and headed south. Alex followed him about twenty yards when he stopped again and pointed to a barely discernable trail that ran back in the direction of the dock and, opposite of that, deeper into the swamp.

"It's not well traveled," Holt said.

"Given the growth rate of swamp foliage, how long do you think it's been since someone used it?"

"I don't know. A month, maybe two."

"But there could also be another trail that is being used on a regular basis."

"Could be. Or it could be that this trail was made by thrill seekers and the old woman is long dead. But we're not going to figure that out standing here." He pointed down the trail that led deep into the swamp. "I think you should take out your gun. Just to be safe."

Alex swallowed and pulled the pistol from the pocket of her backpack. Holt gave her a single nod and strode forward into the darkness.

The sounds of their progress through the swamp seemed to echo in a vacuum of silence. Alex pushed a branch out of her way and collected a spider on the back of her hand for the effort. She shook her hand to fling the spider back out into the swamp, then rubbed her hand on her jeans, certain she could still feel the creature crawling on her hand.

Holt constantly scanned the swamp as they walked, up and down and in every direction. Threats this deep in the bayou were numerous and could come from the ground or from above and all of them deadly. It felt as if they'd been working for hours, but Alex knew it had been only minutes since they'd left the boat.

She knew coming here had been a long shot—a nonshot, really—but she found her spirits waning the deeper they pushed into the swamp. Even if Erika had been here, how could they possibly find a clue in all this?

Just as she was about to call the whole thing off, Holt stopped and turned to her, one finger over his lips. She froze and looked in the direction he pointed to the left of the trail. Just past a thick grouping of cypress trees, she could barely make out the outline of a roof.

Alex nodded, understanding that Holt wanted to make their approach as quiet as possible. He exited the path, cutting straight through the swamp toward the cabin. Slowly and stealthily, they crept closer and closer until they reached the tree line that marked the tiny clearing that the cabin rested in.

Holt lifted his pistol and pointed to hers. Alex removed the safety and clutched the gun with both hands. If she had to shoot, she wanted to make sure it was a steady shot. Holt slipped from behind the wall of cypress trees and hurried over to the wall of the cabin. He pressed his body against the wall, listening for any noise inside, then motioned for her to join him.

Alex edged around the tree and slipped across the open stretch of swamp to join Holt. As soon as she slipped behind him, Holt began moving slowly down the side of the cabin. Fortunately, the cabin contained no windows on this side, so there was no risk of being seen by anyone inside. Unfortunately, Alex was painfully aware of the risk of being heard with every step she made on the dry marsh grass.

When they reached the edge of the cabin, Holt peered around, then slipped around the corner. Alex followed just in time to see him peeking into the front door that already stood wide open. He motioned to her to follow before he stepped inside.

The cabin was one tiny room, no bigger than a basic second bedroom in a house. A cot stood in one corner and a wood-burning stove in the other. A table, made of the bound branches of cypress trees, stood in the center of the room. Shelves covered every square inch of wall space, filled with candles and glass jars. God only knew what was inside of them. On the table sat several ceremonial masks made of leather. Alex had seen replicas in the tourist stores in downtown New Orleans, but she had a feeling these were the real thing.

Alex sucked in a breath and she scanned the room, trying to take it all in. The cabin was dirty, with a layer of dust covering every surface, but clearly someone was still staying here or had stayed here fairly recently. If it had been abandoned, it hadn't been long enough for the place to get completely run-down.

Alex took a step over to the stove and lifted

the lid off a cast-iron pot. She blanched at the putrid smell and quickly replaced the lid.

"Spoiled?" Holt asked.

"I don't think so. I think that abomination was intentional. What in the world goes on here? Look at the candles, the jars of...something. That witch theory is looking a lot more believable."

"It's disconcerting," Holt agreed, "but you know the old ways, even if we don't come from families that practiced them. If the woman has been out here all her life, likely she's deeply set in the old voodoo traditions. That doesn't make her a witch."

Alex crossed her arms across her chest as a chill washed over her. "Something's not right here. More than it just being creepy."

"Well, there doesn't appear to be anything to see, so we may as well leave the creepy and whatever else behind."

Holt took a step toward the open doorway but before he could exit the cabin, a jar from a shelf above the door fell off its perch, exploding on the wooden floor at his feet.

Alex's hand involuntarily flew up and covered her mouth, stifling a cry. Holt's eyes widened as he looked up at the shelf and back down at the floor.

"It must have been near the edge."

Alex scanned the shelves. "None of the other jars are near the edge, we didn't bump anything and there's no wind."

"So what are you saying—that it flew off the shelf by itself?"

"Or maybe something made it. I think we should get out of here, before something more dangerous than a glass jar takes flight."

Holt stared down at the shattered glass, frowning, then he bent over and picked something pink out of the remains of the jar. He held it up to inspect and Alex saw his jaw clench.

"What is it?" Alex asked, already afraid of the answer.

"It's a barrette. Just like the one Erika was wearing when she disappeared."

Alex sucked in a breath. "You're sure?"

Holt nodded and pulled a matching barrette out of his jean's pocket. "It was a set of six matching barrettes. Sarah gave me one…just in case."

Alex took the two barrettes from his hand. "Just in case," she repeated as she stared at the two strips of pink. Holt was right. They were identical.

"What was it doing in that jar?" The pitch of her voice shot up a notch as all sorts of horrible images raced through her mind.

"I don't know," Holt said, his expression grim. "But we're going to find out."

Holt stepped out of the cabin and inspected the ground surrounding the front door. "I can barely make out a set of prints that leads away from the door toward the swamp in that direction." He pointed in the opposite direction of the dock.

The open patch surrounding the cabin suddenly grew darker and they looked up at the sky, beginning to swirl with dark clouds.

"The storm's moving in early," Alex said. "Not good."

"No. This is the last place I want to be trapped in a storm."

"But we're not going to leave, are we?"

Holt stared at the sky, frowning. "We can try to follow the footsteps, but when it starts raining, we have to leave and in a hurry. Any footprints that are visible will be lost in the downpour, anyway."

Alex looked at the swamp, now almost completely dark from the fading sunlight. "Then we'll hurry."

Chapter Five

Two hours later, Holt cursed as rain began pouring from the sky. Two long, sweaty, dirty hours of thrashing through the swamp and they had nothing to show for it. The trail had gone cold thirty minutes before and they'd wandered aimlessly since then, looking for any sign of a person passing through.

"We have to get out of here," Holt said.

"I know," Alex said, the frustration and disappointment evident in her voice.

"With any luck, we'll beat the worst of it. I'm going to move fast, so yell if you fall behind."

He turned toward the dock and started the long walk back through the swamp, stopping only occasionally to ensure they were going the right direction. It took forty-five minutes to reach the cabin and by then, the rain had increased in size and volume and he could hear the sound of thunder in the distance.

He stopped at the cabin long enough to ensure no one had returned, and then gave Alex a once-over. She was a bit winded and had some scratches on her arms, but looked good overall. Too good.

"How are you holding up?" he asked.

Alex took a deep breath and slowly blew it out. "I'm glad I haven't scrimped on my treadmill workout."

"Me, too," Holt said, trying not to think about how good Alex's toned body looked in old jeans and a T-shirt, a sheen of sweat glistening on her bare skin.

Lightning flashed overhead and thunder followed a second later. Alex looked up at the swirling, black clouds and bit her lower lip.

"We're not going to make it," she said.

"We're going to try. Let's go."

By the time they reached the boat, the storm hit full force. The wind whipped across the bayou, scattering the lily pads across the water's surface. Holt jumped in the boat and reached back to offer Alex his hand.

She clutched his hand and placed her first foot into the rocking boat, struggling to maintain her balance. Before she lifted her other leg, a gunshot echoed through the swamp.

The ping of a bullet hitting metal sounded right behind Holt. He yanked Alex into the boat and pushed her to the bottom.

"Stay down!" he yelled and jumped to the back of the boat and started the engine. Alex huddled down in the bottom of the boat and looked up at him, her eyes wide.

A second shot sounded and he felt a burn on his biceps. He threw the boat in reverse and throttled away from the bank so fast that he almost lost his balance. Crouching as low as possible, he threw the boat into Forward and twisted the throttle.

The boat leaped to the top of the water as a third gunshot sounded. A second later, he gave a silent prayer of thanks when he realized the bullet hadn't hit him. Between the rain pouring down his face and the lack of sunlight, his visibility was almost nothing, but the shooter's was also. The farther he moved from the dock, the better their chances that the shooter couldn't land an accurate shot.

He glanced down at Alex, who was clutching the seat, to avoid the worst of the beating that the choppy waves were inflicting on the boat. But he knew that tomorrow, she'd feel this escape on every square inch of her body.

The raindrops stung his face as they raced across the water, and he held one hand in front of his face to block the worst of it. As soon as he rounded the corner out of the shooter's line of sight, he slowed enough to eliminate the worst of the pounding.

Alex pulled herself up from the bottom of the boat and into the seat in front of him.

"Are you okay?" he asked.

She looked back at him and nodded, then her eyes widened. "But you're not. You're bleeding."

He looked down at his biceps, completely forgotten in the rush to get away. Blood stained the sleeve of his T-shirt, the rain diluting it and washing it down his arm.

"I'm fine," he said. "The shot just nicked me." He pointed to a storage bin at the front of the boat. "There should be some slickers in the box."

She pulled two slickers out of the bin and handed one to him. He pulled on the slicker and lowered the hood as far as possible without blocking his vision, then glanced up at the storm and increased his speed a little. The worst was yet to come, and he wanted to be safely tucked between four walls when it hit.

The dock was a good thirty minutes away but with a slight detour, they could be safely indoors in ten minutes. When the channel turned toward the dock, he veered to the right. Alex looked back in surprise but he held up a hand and waved her off. She frowned, and Holt knew she'd already figured out where they were going. She'd been there many times before.

It was the first place they'd ever made love.

Holt shook his head to clear his mind of such thoughts. It did no good to dwell on a past that had no future.

As he pulled up to the dock in front of his cabin, the storm hit full force. Lightning flashed from the sky and struck the earth with such force that the ground trembled. The wind whipped across the bayou so hard it set him off balance as he jumped onto the pier. He grabbed a pylon to steady himself before he fell off the pier and into the tumultuous bayou water, then reached down to help Alex out of the boat.

They ran to the cabin, hunched over in an attempt to hurry through the harsh winds. Holt unlocked the door to the cabin and the wind flung the door open, banging it against the inside wall. The wind swept into the cabin, scattering paper from the kitchen table.

Alex raced inside and he pushed the door shut and secured the dead bolt. "Stay here," he told her and quickly checked the bedroom and bathroom of the tiny cabin for any unwelcome visitors. There was no chance the shooter could have beaten them here, but the shooter might not be working alone.

Alex stood in the middle of the room that

served as kitchen, dining and living area, her arms crossed over her chest. She was soaking wet from head to toe, and still she managed to be the most beautiful woman he'd ever laid eyes on.

"Is everything okay?" she asked.

"Yeah," he said, and handed her one of the clean towels he'd taken from the bathroom. "I can offer you sweats and a T-shirt. They'll be too big, but you should get out of those wet clothes before you get sick."

Alex looked out the window and bit her lower lip. He knew what she'd been hoping for—that he would drive her to Sarah's house—but one look at the raging storm outside and even Alex had to admit that it wasn't safe to drive right now.

"That's fine," she said finally.

"The worst will probably blow over in an hour or so. You're welcome to take a hot shower. I'm going to fix some sandwiches."

Alex stared at him a moment, then blurted out, "Someone was shooting at us. You got hit by a bullet. Are you even going to mention that?"

Holt frowned. "I wasn't planning on it. At least not until I have an idea on the matter."

Alex shook her head. "Well, at least let me

dress that wound while you try to formulate a good idea about someone trying to kill us."

Holt wiped the blood away from the wound on his biceps and realized it was a bit deeper than he'd thought. He nodded to Alex and motioned her into the bathroom.

He'd been back in the cabin only a few weeks, but basic supplies were the first thing he'd acquired. Probably his military training at work. He pulled peroxide and bandages from a linen cabinet and placed them on the counter while Alex grabbed cotton swabs from a jar.

She soaked one of the swabs in peroxide and gently cleaned the wound. "It looks like it just grazed you," she said. "Do you have any anti-bacterial cream?"

He pointed to the top shelf in the cabinet.

She put a clean cotton swab over the wound. "Hold this," she said as she reached for the cream. Then, she pulled his fingers away from the wound. "I think it's stopped bleeding." She squeezed a small amount of cream onto her finger and applied it to the wound, then covered the entire area with a large bandage. "Make sure you change this twice a day. The last thing you want is an infection."

"I know," Holt said, and smiled.

"Oh." She blushed. "That advice must sound stupid to someone who's been at war. I'm sure you're well versed on all the medical risks associated with a bullet wound."

"It's good advice." He stepped closer to her, knowing what he was about to do was a really bad idea, but unable to come up with one good reason not to.

He pulled her close to him in one sudden motion that made her gasp. Before he could change his mind, he lowered his lips to hers.

Her lips were soft, as he'd remembered, but her body was different, better. The curves that pressed against him screamed *woman* instead of *girl,* and his body responded in kind. It was as if ten years had melted away and they were again teenagers who'd skipped class to spend time alone at the cabin.

Immediately she pushed back and stared at him, her eyes wide. "I think I'll wait in the truck," she said as she whirled around and fled the bathroom.

"It's not safe out there," he said, following her into the living area.

"It's safer than being in here." She slipped out the front door and back into the raging storm.

ALEX SLAMMED THE TRUCK DOOR and crossed her arms, shivering. *Stupid,* she chided herself as she stared into the downpour. *You're running like a teenager.*

But she couldn't shake the unnerved feeling she had from the kiss. Her skin was still on fire everywhere Holt's body had made contact with hers. Her pulse raced and she felt as if it would leap from her chest. If asked, she'd swear she'd been less stressed when someone was shooting at her.

Minutes later Holt slid into the truck, fully dressed and wearing a rain slicker. He handed Alex a blanket and started the truck without even a glance in her direction. Alex cast a sideways look at him, trying to gauge his mood. The anger she expected to see wasn't there. Instead, he looked pensive and worried.

She sighed, annoyed with herself.

Her niece was missing and Holt had been shot, but here she was, worrying that he was busy dwelling on her rejection of him. What an ego she'd developed as an adult.

Holt made the short drive in complete silence, and Alex wasn't sure whether to be disappointed or relieved that he wasn't going to talk about the obvious issues that still lingered between them. She finally settled on relieved, already having entirely too much to process for the day.

He pulled up to the curb of Sarah's house and walked around to open her door.

"I'll look into some things in the morning," he said. "Make sure the house is locked up tight."

She nodded and hurried up the walk to the house, afraid to say a word lest things she didn't want to address came falling out. She slipped inside the house, locked the door and drew the dead bolt. Lifting a slat of the miniblinds, she peered out the front window into the storm and watched as the taillights of Holt's truck faded into the distance.

She, of all people, had the skill set to handle conflict. From now on she'd concentrate only on finding Erika. When she was safely back in New Orleans, she'd have plenty of time to address her apparently unresolved feelings for Holt Chamberlain.

ALEX WALKED OUT OF Sarah's guest bathroom, still toasty from the steaming hot shower she'd taken. Sarah was perched on the edge of the bed, anxiously awaiting a recount of the day's events, and she jumped up when Alex exited the bathroom.

"I made gumbo," Sarah said. "Too nervous to rest, I guess, and it's a good thing, since you showed up looking like a drowned rat. Are you okay? Do you need warmer clothes?"

Alex placed one hand on Sarah's arm. "I'm fine. Take a deep breath. We're going to go downstairs and fix two bowls of your fabulous gumbo, and I'm going to tell you everything."

Sarah blew out a breath. "I know you are. I'm sorry, Alex. I'm just so jumpy."

Alex gave her cousin a hug. "I know, honey. You have every right to be, but we're going to fix this. We're going to find Erika."

Sarah gave her a small smile and nodded. "I trust you. You know I trust you. All our lives, you've always been the one to fix things. It's just that this is so much bigger than anything else."

Alex placed one arm around her cousin's shoulders and pulled her out of the room and into the kitchen. "So we'll work harder."

They fixed bowls of gumbo and sat at the small table in the breakfast nook. Alex recounted to Sarah how they found the dock and then the cabin. She described what they'd found in the cabin, leaving no detail out of her story. The truth was scary, but Sarah deserved to know everything.

"As we were leaving," Alex said, "a jar on one of the shelves over the door fell right in front of us."

Sarah's eyes widened. "How?"

"I don't know and don't even want to guess." Alex took a deep breath. "There was a pink barrette inside the jar. Just like the ones Erika was wearing."

Sarah sucked in a breath. "Oh, my God. My poor baby. She's there with that witch woman. I knew it. I told you there was no other explanation."

"It looks suspicious," Alex said, trying to keep her cousin from getting worked up to the point of uselessness. "We followed a trail away from the cabin until the storm hit, and then we had to turn back. I'm sorry, but the barrette is all we found."

Sarah stared down into her gumbo for a couple of seconds, then frowned. "That's it? Then why did Holt bring you home in his truck? Why didn't you return to the dock and get your car?"

"Holt docked at his cabin to get us out of the storm. We were too deep in the swamp to beat it."

Sarah narrowed her eyes at Alex. "You're not telling me something. I know you. You're not lying, but you're leaving something out."

Alex sighed. "Someone shot at us as we were leaving the bank of the island. One of the bullets grazed Holt's arm, but he's fine."

Sarah jumped up from the table, her eyes wide with fear. "Someone tried to kill you? You walked in my house, took a shower and sat here eating gumbo knowing that someone tried to kill you just hours before? Are you sure I'm the one with mental problems?"

"What do you want me to tell you—that I'm moving through a logical, rational routine hoping to make sense of it all? Hoping that it will prevent me from breaking down at a time when you need me to be a rock?"

Sarah slid back into her chair and Alex reached across the table to cover her cousin's hand with her own.

"I'm scared, Sarah. Really scared. When we were trying to get away, I didn't have much time to think about it, but afterward…well, let's just say I'm not the rock you think I am."

Alex's mind flashed back to Holt's cabin. His hard, muscular body pressed against her. The touch of his lips on hers. The heat between them that wasn't coming just from their contact.

A killer and Holt Chamberlain.

She wasn't sure which scared her more.

Chapter Six

Holt stepped into the sheriff's office the next morning, still cursing himself for the day before. The whole thing had been one giant mistake, beginning with going to that island and ending with kissing Alex. But if he was going to be honest with himself, he'd do it all over again if he had to. Finding Erika was a priority. Kissing Alex wasn't nearly as important as finding a missing child, but the urgency he'd felt when he kissed her in the cabin the day before had been no less than that he'd felt when fleeing the shooter.

Which was rather appropriate when he considered that loving Alex was just as deadly as being shot. He hadn't even been in her company for a full day, and he'd already made a move on her. Ten years in the desert and it had all been a waste of time.

Since he was early, he started a pot of coffee and headed to his office. He needed to do some research on the island. With any luck, he'd be able to find out more about the old woman who lived there. Even if she'd been born in the bayou with no hospital records, the land had to be deeded to someone. He also needed to pull all the files from the cases thirty-six years ago.

He hadn't even been born when the girls went missing, but the story had been passed down through generations of families in Vodoun. The police would have investigated the old woman back then. Maybe he'd be able to find something in the old files that he could use. Some clue to help him find Erika.

He turned on the computer and began a search of the land records. By the time he'd finished his first cup of coffee, he had his answer. The name on the deed was Mathilde Tregre. He let himself into the storage room, pulled the boxes from the old kidnappings and carted them back to his office. The interview with the woman was in the first box.

The woman wasn't listed as Mathilde or Tregre. She'd claimed her name was t'Mat. That made sense, given the old custom of naming a daughter after her mother and using the *t* in front of the name or shortened name to mean "little." In this case, "Little Mathilde." Holt poured himself another cup of coffee and settled into his chair to read over the interview.

Mathilde had been clear from the start that she hadn't seen the girls on the island or anywhere else, despite personal items belonging to the girls that were found on her property. She also claimed that this visit to the sheriff's department was the first time in over a year that she'd been off the island. Based on the question marks drawn in pencil around the typewritten transcript, it was clear that the old sheriff hadn't believed her, but he didn't have any good reason to hold her.

So he'd let her go.

According to his mother, the people in Vodoun had made their displeasure more than apparent. She said the anxiety level in the town was unlike anything she'd ever seen. She'd been a teen herself at the time and remembered not being allowed to go outside unless her mother was with her. The shops in town were almost empty, the streets vacant. Some people even kept their kids out of school and church.

As the weeks passed, and no more children went missing, the town slowly returned to its normal routine. And the case went cold.

Had Mathilde Tregre taken those girls? And if she had, why wait thirty-six years before claiming another victim? Everything in him screamed that this was wrong—that they'd missed something then and he was missing something now. But he had no idea what.

He closed the folder and sat back, frustrated with all the information that only created more questions. The facts of the cases were simple: thirty-six years ago, three girls had disappeared from Vodoun, and now Erika. There was no reason, save the doll and the past presumption that Mathilde was somehow involved, to assume the two were related. But if one did assume they were related, then the logical explanation was that the same person had committed both crimes.

If he assumed that the same person had committed both crimes, and that person wasn't Mathilde Tregre, then that meant the perpetrator had either moved away and just returned or had been in prison and was recently released. If they'd been living somewhere else for thirty-six years, Holt had no doubt that similar cases would crop up in the national database.

He accessed the national database for missing children and put in the case information for Erika and the girls from thirty-six years before. Then he ran a query on all inmates that had been released from prison that year that had been in for crimes involving children. The national database would take a while to process, but his prisoner query was back in minutes, listing two men recently paroled after serving on pedophilia charges. Both were listed at New Orleans addresses. A quick query returned the name of the parole officer that both men shared.

Holt checked his watch. Only seven a.m., but there was still a chance the PO would answer a call. On the fifth ring, he was about to give up, when a sleepy voice answered. Holt explained to the man who he was and why he was calling and the sleepiness left his voice almost immediately.

"Give me a minute to get to my computer," the man said.

Holt heard the sound of doors opening and an office chair squeaking. A couple of minutes later, the parole officer was back on the line. "Both men clocked into their construction jobs every morning this week at eight a.m. and didn't leave until six p.m."

"How reliable is the foreman tracking their time?"

"Very. The guy was a fourth-generation cop who retired into his uncle's business. If the cons have any construction skills, he puts them to work for me, hoping they'll turn around and not go back in when they see they can make a good living with honest work. He's been pretty successful."

"Lunch hour?"

"Only thirty minutes and they bring food in for the workers. And the job they're working is on the south side of New Orleans. They couldn't even make it to Vodoun in thirty minutes, much less back to the site to clock in."

Holt sighed. "I agree. Thanks for the information."

"I'll ask around. If I come up with anything, I'll let you know. I'm really sorry you caught this. I hate the kid cases."

"Me, too," Holt said, and hung up the phone.

He stared out the window and frowned. Just because those two guys were accounted for didn't mean it wasn't an ex-con. It could have been one paroled outside of the area. Someone with a friend or relative to visit close by that had run across Erika by chance and took her.

But that didn't explain where the doll came from.

And that was the big fly in the investigative ointment. That doll implied planning and plotting. That doll meant everything had been premeditated, and *that* meant someone had been watching for a while, just waiting for the right opportunity.

Which meant someone local.

Holt shoved the chair back and left the office, certain he needed another cup of coffee before he compiled a list of every Vodoun resident and started crossing them off one at a time. He'd barely made it back to his desk before the phone started ringing. One glance at the display told him he wasn't going to like the call. It was his uncle, and Holt could think of only one reason why he'd be calling the sheriff's department this early.

"Morning, Jasper," Holt answered.

"What the hell were you thinking taking the department's boat and running around the bayou over some nonsense cooked up by a crazy woman? I called the office trying to find you and the dispatcher told me everything, so don't even try to deny it."

"I'm not trying to deny it. Sarah is convinced her daughter was taken by the woman on the island. Either I checked it out or she was going to."

"Then let her do it. It's not your job."

"No, it's yours. Last time I checked, the department was supposed to investigate the disappearance of children. That's what I'm doing. I'm assuming you wouldn't want two missing people in Vodoun, and that's exactly what we'd have if Sarah went into the swamp alone."

"That woman is a waste of this town's time and resources."

"It wasn't a waste."

There was dead silence for a moment, then

his uncle responded. "Don't tell me you found something."

"We found a barrette. Like the ones Erika was wearing when she disappeared."

"So what? Dime-store barrettes are hardly evidence that the girl was there. It could have been dropped by anyone."

"Yeah, but this particular barrette happened to be in a glass jar on a shelf in the old woman's cabin. That seems awful strange to me."

His uncle cursed again, and Holt knew he was more than pissed that the whole thing hadn't been the exercise in futility he'd assumed it was. With this evidence, his uncle had no choice but to authorize a full search of the island. Of course, a full search in Vodoun meant Holt and whoever else he could muster up to help. But there was the not-so-small issue of someone shooting at them to be taken into consideration before he started letting people volunteer.

"There's more," Holt said.

"What now?"

Holt told him about the shooter, glossing over just how close their escape had been.

"It must have been the old woman, right?" his uncle asked.

"That's the logical answer, but what if it wasn't? We don't really know all that much about the woman. All these years she's been out in that swamp, and yet people in Vodoun have only seen her a handful of times and her mother a handful before that. Some have never seen her at all. How do we know she doesn't have a husband or kids or other family living out there with her?"

"We don't, which is all the more reason not to run out into the swamp half-cocked and with a civilian. Especially that particular civilian. What were you thinking, bringing Alex with you?"

"It was the only way we could get Sarah to stay put. With her emotions running high, Sarah would have been a big liability. Alex was the better choice if one of them had to go."

"And what about Bobby? I still think he took the girl. Surely someone's got a line on him by now."

"He hasn't been sighted at the border, and there's been no activity on his bank account or credit cards." Holt recounted the story Bobby's neighbor had told him about the movers. "It doesn't feel right."

"Well, if he was going to kidnap his kid and make a run for it, he'd hardly do it in the middle of the day when someone could easily see him and mention the moving truck to Sarah."

"I guess," Holt said, still feeling that Bobby

was the wrong direction to look. "I'll follow up. Try to find the moving truck."

"I don't suppose I have to tell you not to set foot on that island again without a warrant. And it's going to take at least a day to get one. I mean it, Holt. Not one foot, or I'll get out of this bed and toss you in jail myself."

Holt looked out the window at the blinding sheets of rain blowing across the parking lot. "No problem," he said, thinking that was likely going to be the easiest thing he agreed to that day.

"I'll get a warrant, but I want your attention focused on finding Bobby. Is that clear?"

"Crystal."

A SCRATCHING NOISE AT THE window woke up Alex, and she bolted upright in bed. It took her a minute to remember she was in the guest room at Sarah's house, and once she did, everything that had happened over the past twenty-four hours came flooding back.

No light crept through the bedroom window, so she knew it wasn't yet dawn. She also knew that Sarah took great care in her landscaping, and that no hedges or trees would be allowed to extend close enough to the house to scrape the sides. There was no plausible explanation for the sound that had wakened her.

She sat stock-still, wondering if perhaps she'd been dreaming. Perhaps her mind had been playing tricks on her, but just as she was about to climb out of bed, she heard it again—a faint scratching sound, like the sound of something sharp and hard rubbing against the window pane.

She slid out of bed, hoping the hardwood floors didn't creak as she slipped over to the window. Easing the heavy curtain to the side a tiny bit, she peered outside into the darkness. The scratching noise sounded again, this time directly in front of her. She raised her gaze just above eye level and that was when she saw him.

The crow.

He was sitting on the branch of a tree, about a foot from the house, staring at her with those black eyes. She brought her hand up over her mouth to stifle a cry. Her pulse spiked and she took a step back from the window, dropping the drape back in place.

But she could still feel its eyes on her.

"It's there, isn't it?" Sarah's voice sounded from the doorway, causing her to jump. "The crow. You saw it."

There was no point in lying. Alex was certain the look on her face had already given everything away.

"On a branch just outside the window."

"It's toying with us," Sarah said, a blush rising up her neck and onto her face. "Bring my baby back!" She strode across the bedroom and yanked the drape completely back.

Alex gasped in horror as Sarah screamed.

The doll Alex had seen on the island sat on the branch where the crow used to be.

Alex grabbed Sarah's hand and pulled her cousin out of the room. She had no idea what to do, but knew she couldn't get her head right with the doll staring at her. Before she could change her mind, she grabbed her cell phone from the kitchen counter and pressed in Holt's number.

"Get to Sarah's house quick," she said.

"On my way," Holt said, and disconnected the call without question.

Sarah stood in the middle of the kitchen, her body taut, her expression full of fear. "What's happening to my baby?" Sarah wailed, and started to sob.

Alex gathered her cousin in her arms and stood there in the middle of the kitchen, rocking her and trying to soothe her, but having absolutely no idea what to say. The reality was, Alex was scared, more scared than she'd ever been before.

Except for that summer.

Everything seemed to come back around to

that summer, no matter how much she tried to push it aside. She'd never faced it before. Had pushed it far down in her memory, pretending it didn't matter since it was so long ago. Now, it had come back to roost. And at the time that Sarah needed her to keep it together the most, she was lost.

It took Holt less than ten minutes to arrive, which told Alex that he'd already been awake, dressed and somewhere other than his cabin when she called. Apparently, a good night's sleep wasn't going any better for Holt than it had for her.

"What's wrong?" he asked, as soon as she opened the front door.

Alex waved him in and looked over at Sarah, who she'd finally gotten settled at the breakfast table with a cup of tea. Her cousin's pale skin and sunken eyes worried her. Sarah couldn't afford to let her health slide, but Alex didn't know how to alleviate her worry. Especially now that she was as worried as Sarah.

"Follow me," she said, and headed down the hall toward the bedroom, Holt close on her heels.

As soon as they were out of earshot of the kitchen, she gave Holt a recount of the morning's events. He looked a bit irritated when she told him about the crow, and Alex knew he thought he'd been summoned here for a bit of overactive imagination, but when she told him about the doll, his jaw set in a hard line and he pushed past her to the window, flinging the drapes back.

The doll, soaked with rain, sat on the branch of the tree, its black eyes staring at them. Holt muttered a low curse and strode down the hall, out of the house and into the storm.

Alex followed him around the house to the window. He stood about ten feet from the tree, studying the ground beneath it.

"No footprints," he said.

Alex held one hand over her forehead to shield her eyes from the rain. "Could the rain have washed them away that quickly? I know it's pouring, but—"

"Are you sure the doll wasn't already in the tree the first time you looked out?"

"I think I know the difference between a crow and a doll," she said, glaring at him.

"I know. Never mind." He pulled a digital camera from his jeans pocket and took a couple of photos, then pulled on a pair of gloves and carefully removed the doll from the tree.

"I have evidence bags in my truck," he said. "Let me get this situated and I'll be inside."

Alex nodded and hurried back into the house, happy that Holt was smart enough not to bring the doll inside the house where Sarah could see it and freak out all over again.

"You're dripping on the floor," Sarah said, as she entered the kitchen. Her voice was flat and vacant, and she stared at the puddles collecting on the floor beneath Alex's robe as if mesmerized.

"I'm sorry." Suddenly Alex felt self-conscious about her thin, wet robe. "I'll be right back."

She hurried to the guest bedroom and threw on a pair of jeans and a T-shirt, then hung her bathrobe in the shower to dry. Holt was already in the kitchen, sitting at the table across from Sarah, when she got there.

"You didn't see or hear anything?" Holt asked Sarah.

Sarah shook her head. "Just Alex when she awakened. I came into her room to tell her I'd make pancakes. She's always loved my blueberry pancakes. Did she ever tell you about the time we ate fifteen of them one Saturday morning?"

"No."

Sarah smiled. "We couldn't play kickball with the other kids, our stomachs were so swollen, but Alex always says my pancakes were worth it. Right?"

Sarah looked up at Alex, the smile seemingly affixed on her face. Alex forced a smile for her cousin and nodded. "Your pancakes are the best in the world."

She looked over at Holt, who shot her a worried look. It was as Alex had feared—Sarah seemed to be breaking with reality.

"Sarah," Alex said. "Do you have an extra blanket? I got a little chilly last night."

"Sure. I have some extras in my bedroom closet."

"Would you mind getting me one and leaving it on my bed? Just in case I have to leave and you're asleep when I get back? I don't want to have to wake you."

Sarah rose from the table and walked down the hall as if programmed to do so.

"This is so not good," Alex said.

"She's disassociating," Holt said, as he watched her cousin walk away.

"Yes. I was hoping to keep her calm and focused, but it's too much for her. The deal with Bobby and now Erika missing. And all the weirdness surrounding it."

Holt frowned. "I know this is going to make you angry, but I wouldn't be doing my job if I didn't ask…"

"You want to know if I think it's possible that Sarah hurt Erika."

Holt stared at her, clearly surprised.

"Part of my work is with mental patients who got commitment instead of incarceration. I've seen and heard horrible things. I know how dark a place the mind can be."

Holt sighed. "I suppose you do."

"But the answer is still no. I don't believe Sarah hurt her daughter."

"But you agree she's capable of it?"

"We're all capable of it. We're human. But that's not what happened here. Sarah was completely lucid when I arrived yesterday. Her condition was normal given the situation, and I saw no indicators that there was a problem with her stability."

"And now?"

"I think we better find Erika before I lose two family members in one week."

Holt started to comment, but Sarah's home telephone interrupted him. Alex jumped up from the table, not wanting her cousin to answer any calls in her current state of mind.

"Is this Mrs. Rhonaldo?"

Alex frowned, not recognizing the voice. "This is her cousin. Mrs. Rhonaldo is ill right now. Can I help you with something?"

"Yes, ma'am. I hope so. This is Al Johnson and I own a pawn shop in New Orleans. Mrs. Rhonaldo's husband sold me a guitar yesterday and I wanted to verify that he was the only owner. It's worth more that way."

Alex gripped the phone so hard her knuckles ached. Bobby owned only one guitar that was worth enough money to pawn, and the only thing he loved more than the instrument was his daughter.

"Mr. Johnson, could you hold for just a moment, please?" Alex covered the phone with her hand and repeated what the pawn shop owner had told her.

Holt jumped up from his seat and reached for the phone. "Mr. Johnson, this is Holt Chamberlain with the Vodoun Sheriff's Department. Mr. Rhonaldo is currently missing, as is his six-year old daughter. Do you have security cameras in your shop?"

Holt nodded to Alex and she felt her pulse increase.

"Could you please pull the tape from when Mr. Rhonaldo sold you the guitar and hold the tape and the guitar until I get there? Thank you."

Holt hung the phone up and pulled his keys from his pocket. "I'll let you know what I find out," he said.

"Wait," Alex said, "I'm going with you."

"No, you're not."

"You haven't lived in Vodoun for ten years.

You may not recognize whoever is on that tape."

"You mean, if it's not Bobby."

"I'd bet everything I own it's not Bobby. There's no way he'd part with that guitar. Not if he were alive." As the words slipped from her mouth, the reality of them sank in and Alex sucked in a breath.

"What about Sarah? Is it safe to leave her alone?"

"A group of ladies from the church are coming over to bring food and have prayer. I'll make sure someone can keep her company until we get back."

"If you think it's okay…"

"Let me check on Sarah." She hurried down the hall before her mind could whirl down a million paths she wasn't ready to take.

Chapter Seven

Holt held the door of the pawn shop open so that Alex could step inside. A big man behind the counter waved as they entered. Holt pulled his badge from his pocket and flashed it as they stepped up to the counter.

The man looked over at a young kid working on a stereo in the corner. "Watch the counter for me, Tim. I need to speak to these people for a minute."

The boy nodded and Al motioned them behind the counter and into an office. Alex glanced at the guitar on his desktop and nodded.

"That's Bobby's guitar," Alex said. "The artwork is custom. There's no two alike." She pulled her wallet from her purse and showed Al a picture of Sarah and Bobby. "Is this the man who sold you the guitar?"

"Not even close," Al said.

"You're sure?" Holt asked.

Al nodded. "In my business, it pays to re-member faces. The guy who sold me the guitar was older, his hair lighter. His eyes were wider set and his nose had been broken before, prob-ably more than once. I used to box, so I know the look."

Holt tried to control his excitement at the first possibility of a decent lead. "Do you think you can work with a sketch artist to get a com-posite of the man?"

"Ain't no need." Al pointed to one of the monitors on his desk. "This is the one that's got the footage you want to see. Real up close and personal."

Holt and Alex leaned over the desk for a closer look at the monitor. At first, it was just Al standing behind the counter, working on a broken jigsaw, then a shadow appeared on the counter and a man stepped up.

Holt struggled to contain his disappointment. "The camera only catches him from behind?"

"Wait a minute," Al said. "They're on rota-tion. The frame will switch to the camera be-hind the counter in a couple of seconds."

Sure enough, a couple of seconds later, the monitor blinked and the view switched to one from behind the counter. Holt studied the man's face, but was certain he'd never seen him before.

"Well?" Al asked.

"You gave a great description," Holt said, "and that's certainly not Bobby. Unfortunately, I've never seen that man before."

Alex shook her head. "Me, either."

"This Bobby," Al said, "is he in some kind of trouble?"

"It's beginning to look like it. His six-year old daughter went missing two days ago. Bobby and his wife are recently separated, and when someone went to question him about the missing girl, they found his place empty."

Al frowned. "That doesn't sound good. I got a little girl myself. Anything happens to her... well, let's just say no man wants to be on the other end of that."

Holt nodded. "I totally agree."

"You can take the guitar. It's likely stolen goods and that's the cost of doing business sometimes."

"I appreciate it," Holt said. He was just about to turn away when the man selling the guitar pulled his right hand out of his jean's pocket and reached for a pen on the counter. Holt stared at the monitor, his pulse ticking up with every second.

The man had the eye tattoo on the back of his hand.

"Can I take the video with me, too?" Holt

asked. "I'd like to run this guy through the system and see if I come up with anything."

"Of course." Al pulled the tape from the VCR and handed it to Holt. "Hey, man, would you mind letting me know when you find that little girl? It'll be on my mind…"

"Sure," Holt said. "Thanks for everything."

He left the office and exited the pawn shop, Alex trailing behind. He was trying to control his warring emotions and thought he was doing a pretty fine job of it.

"So are you going to tell me what happened in there?" Alex asked.

"What do you mean?"

"You looked like you'd seen a ghost right before Al turned off that tape."

He held in a groan. Why did he think for one minute that Alex would fail to notice something like that? She'd noticed everything when they were kids, and now she had a PhD and a job that required her to notice the little things.

"It's nothing," he said.

"It didn't seem like nothing. Look, if you know something about this man that will help us find Erika, you have to tell me."

"It has nothing to do with Erika."

"Then what—"

"That's not up for discussion." He strode past her and crossed the street, leaving her standing on the corner, staring after him. He wasn't ready to discuss the man yet. And certainly not with Alex. Seeing her had already brought back too many uncertainties, too many questions.

It seemed to Holt that the entire life he'd run to escape was unraveling right before his eyes.

ALEX PUSHED HER SHOPPING CART down the aisle of the Vodoun Sack-a-lot, trying to concentrate on buying food for Sarah's house. So far, she'd picked up a tube of toothpaste, a bottle of cooking oil and matches. As long as they wanted to have good breath while setting the house on fire, they were set.

And now she was on the spice aisle, with not a vegetable or meat product in her cart to season. She shook her head and pushed the cart to the end of the aisle, determined to find something easy to fix that was also edible.

She was eyeing the meat counter when she pushed her cart out of the aisle and another shopper crashed into her from the side.

"I'm so sorry," Alex said immediately, then looked over to see the very annoyed face of her least favorite woman in Vodoun—Lorraine Conroy, the sheriff's mother.

"Well, I've always thought it," Lorraine said, studying one of her perfectly manicured nails, "but it's quite refreshing to actually hear you say it."

"If I'd known it was you on the other end, I wouldn't have apologized. I would have shoved the cart harder. Did you break a nail? Do you want me to call Care Flight?"

Lorraine shook her head, the condescending expression she wore one born of constant practice. "Your mother never did manage to teach you manners, did she?"

"My mother taught me that manners only apply in our actions toward human beings." She smiled.

"Cute," Lorraine said, and dropped her hand. "I suppose you're here to fix the latest mess that trashy cousin of yours has gotten herself into."

Alex felt the blood rush to her face. It was one thing for Lorraine to direct her hostility on Alex. That was nothing new. But she wasn't going to let the woman disparage her cousin's plight.

"Her daughter is missing. I would think that even you would find a missing child disturbing."

Lorraine laughed. "Well, dear, you've already pointed out that I'm not human. Besides, everyone knows that foreign husband of hers took the child. Why all the fuss? She's probably much better off with him in whatever country that is than being raised by Sarah."

"You're despicable."

"No, what's despicable is that trash like Sarah is allowed to live in such a nice place like Vodoun. Marrying that foreigner and bringing him here, having a child with him. She was asking for something like this to happen. Why, that sort of thing is all over the television."

Alex clenched the handle of the shopping cart, certain that if she freed up a hand, she wouldn't be able to stop herself from slapping the smug look right off Lorraine's face.

"You *are* here to take care of Sarah, right?" Lorraine asked. "I mean, certainly you didn't come running back here to take another stab at hooking Holt. Because we all know how that turned out the first time. It's one thing to embarrass yourself by throwing yourself at a man when you're twenty, but it's really pathetic when you're in your thirties."

"But throwing yourself at a much younger man at—shall we be polite and say sixty—is perfectly acceptable." Everyone in Vodoun knew that Lorraine had taken up with a much younger man after her much older husband's death. Lorraine claimed he was a business partner, but no one in Vodoun was buying it.

"Business is a totally different issue." She

narrowed her eyes at Alex. "But then, maybe this *is* business. I'm sure by now you know Holt's trust fund was turned over to him when he turned thirty. I guess the fact that he ran off to Iraq to get away from you hasn't deterred you from your goal."

Alex felt the blood rush up her face, causing her temples to throb. "You have the nerve to accuse me of chasing after Holt for his money? You married a man twice your age just to double your holdings."

Lorraine laughed. "My husband wasn't useful for much of anything, really, but making money. Making money was the one thing he did without fail."

"That wasn't the *only* thing he did without fail, was it, Lorraine?" Her husband's reputation as a philanderer was also common knowledge.

Lorraine glared, her face flushing red with anger. "I suppose it takes a whore to know one."

Alex slipped one hand from the shopping cart and started to step around when a hand clasped her shoulder and squeezed.

"That's quite enough, Lorraine," Holt said. "I would expect a woman of your caliber to show more class than this."

"What do you know about class, Holt Chamberlain? You certainly didn't learn anything from your father, and your mother's always been a fool."

Lorraine whirled her shopping cart around and took off toward the checkout counter.

"Why do I let that woman get to me?" Alex asked. "I'm so mad, my hands are shaking."

"Lorraine is the biggest bitch ever to walk Vodoun. She gets to everyone. I would apologize for her, but I stopped taking responsibility for things my family did years ago."

Alex sighed. "It's not your place to apologize, although it's likely the only one I'd ever get."

"Likely," Holt agreed. "How's Sarah?"

"Not good. She was painting the garage when I left—with red nail polish. She insisted I buy more because she needs enough to finish the trim."

Holt glanced down at her shopping cart. "So you thought you'd burn down the garage once she was done? I'm not sure where the toothpaste fits into that."

Alex laughed. "I was thinking the same thing earlier. I'm supposed to be picking up groceries, but my concentration is off."

"Let me help."

Alex stared. "You?"

"I make a mean spaghetti sauce. That should last you guys a couple of days."

Alex felt a flicker of warmth in her heart and

tried to squelch it. "You don't have to do that. We'll manage."

"I want to. Look, I already feel like I'm not doing enough. This storm will break tonight, and with any luck we can go back to the island tomorrow, but I feel like I ought to be doing more. I'm not made for sitting still."

Alex knew she should say no. Every square inch of her body screamed at her that spending a domestic evening with Holt was just asking for trouble. But she found herself nodding, despite every completely reasonable argument to the contrary that she could summon.

"I'll meet you there in a half hour," Holt said, and walked away.

Alex watched after him, her mind whirling with a million thoughts. Where was Erika? What had happened to Bobby? Who was the man who'd sold Bobby's guitar and what did Holt know about it?

Spaghetti.

Damn. Alex scanned the store, but didn't see the top of Holt's head in any of the aisles. What the heck did you buy to make spaghetti?

SARAH PULLED A FIFTH BAG of tomatoes from the shopping bags that Alex had placed on the counter. Five bags. Five different types of tomatoes. She looked over at Alex, eyebrows raised.

"Are we cooking spaghetti for a very picky group of eaters, or is there some sort of spaghetti cook-off happening here that you didn't tell me about?"

Alex looked over at the counter and held in a groan. "I might have invited Holt for dinner."

"You might have? How much does he plan on eating?"

"I had a run-in with Lorraine in the supermarket, and Holt interrupted right about when I was going to clock her—"

"That man's always had horrible timing."

Alex stared at Sarah for a moment, then burst out laughing. "Oh, my God," she said and grabbed a paper towel to wipe the tears running down her cheeks. "Oh, Sarah. You don't know how good it is to hear you sound so normal."

"Well, if I'd known it was going to make you hysterical, I would have kept my mouth shut."

Alex threw her arms around Sarah and gave her a squeeze. "We're going to make it through this."

"I know."

Alex pushed back and gave Sarah a close look. Her cousin's color had returned and her expression was almost serene. "What happened to change you like this? I know the medicine didn't do it. It's not that powerful. Did you sniff too much fingernail polish when you were painting the garage?"

"I talked to Madam Fredericks after you left for the grocery store."

"The palm reader on Main Street?"

Sarah nodded. "I know you don't believe in the old ways, but I think we should take every avenue available to us. Madam Fredericks has been right in everything she's told me so far. She's going to be right again."

Alex bit her bottom lip, trying to formulate a response. "What did she say?"

"She said Erika would be returned to me."

Alex frowned. "Is that it?"

"Yes," Sarah said, and smiled. "Don't you see, Alex? My baby is going to come back to me."

Alex nodded and forced a smile. "That's great. Really great, Sarah."

"So help me wash the dishes and I can tell you the gossip about Lorraine and that 'business associate' of hers."

"I really should check my messages at the hospital," Alex said, certain that Lorraine was the last person she wanted to talk about at the moment.

"C'mon. It will be just like old times—you and me talking trash about that bitch." Sarah grinned.

"Well, when you put it that way."

Sarah hurried to the kitchen and tossed a dishrag to Alex. "I know you're just dying to hear about how she took him as her date to the party at the country club last week."

Alex lifted the dishrag off her shoulder and hurried to the sink next to Sarah. "The country club? Did he burst into flames when he stepped across the hallowed, rich-people-only threshold?"

"No, Satan's mistress must have provided him some form of immunity."

"But surely everyone is talking? What was she thinking? I mean, as much as I can't stand Lorraine, I've never thought she was foolish."

"It's a mixed bag. The men think she's an old lady acting like a fool with a young man. And they would know as most of the country club men are on their second or third wives, all younger than their children. The women are a different story."

"How's that?"

"Some think she's a shameful hussy. This is still the Bible Belt, after all. But a lot think it's about time that 'more mature' women took advantage of the same opportunities as men."

"How very progressive of the ladies of Vodoun."

Sarah waved a hand in dismissal. "Oh, the

older ones all think she looks a fool, but the girls in their teens and twenties think it's cool."

"Still, what does anyone know about the man? I mean, he's been around for years, but always lurking in the shadows. I don't even know his name."

"Martin Rommel. And I'd bet anything I own that our good Sheriff Conroy had him checked out long ago. If there was anything there that he could use to get rid of the guy, he would have."

"True, but you're also talking about Jasper, who probably couldn't find anything on the man if he was holding a smoking gun over a body. Still, I guess it's not exactly pleasant to have your mother running around with a guy your age or younger."

"Not to mention the fear of lost fortune. I mean, what if she went off her trolley and married him? Jasper could get cut out of everything."

"Do you think that's what this Martin Rommel is up to?"

"Well, don't you? I mean, why else would a young, good-looking man want to take up with a woman old enough to draw Social Security? Especially someone as nasty as Lorraine."

"You have a very valid point." And what Sarah said made sense, but something still didn't feel quite right to Alex. Maybe it was because she knew better than anyone just how shrewd Lorraine was. Would the nemesis of all decent women actually stoop to paying for the company of a man?

"You know what I never understood," Alex said.

"You don't understand something?" Sarah teased.

Alex smiled. "This animosity that Lorraine has for your mom. I used to think it was a child-hood thing, but surely she would have outgrown it. There have to be a million other adult slights more important to her by this time. So why all the vitriol?"

Sarah shook her head. "I had a run-in with her about a month ago at the post office. I'd stopped there on my way to see Mom, and was still fighting mad when I got to the nursing home. You know how when we'd ask her about it when we were kids, she always made up some fantastic excuse?"

"Like the cat drank the last of her cereal milk."

"Exactly. Well, I figured Mom's not as sharp as she used to be and she doesn't work as hard to control her tongue…"

"So you asked again. Very sneaky and very like you. Did you get an answer?"

Sarah frowned. "Not really. She said that Lorraine hated all the pretty girls because her husband liked them too much."

"We already knew that. Everyone in Vodoun knows that."

"I know, but that's all I could get out of her. And she was serious when she said it." Sarah turned to face Alex. "Do you think he could have hit on Mom?"

"I think he hit on everything female within a hundred-mile radius. And your mom is gorgeous. It wouldn't surprise me."

"But she was already married when she moved to Vodoun."

"So was he."

Sarah rolled her eyes. "A valid point."

She handed Alex the last dish and shook the water from her hands. "I better go put on a nice shirt. Since we're having company. And who knows? Tonight may be the night Erika returns."

Alex watched as Sarah strode down the hall to her bedroom. She'd been happy and surprised to see her cousin with improved spirits, but her emotions were completely mixed on the reason. Logic and an education in science told Alex the old ways weren't possible, but an upbringing mired in lore and tradition always left that tiny bit of what-if in the back of her mind.

What troubled Alex the most was the prediction itself. Madam Fredericks had stated Erika would be returned to Sarah. But she hadn't stated that Erika would be returned alive.

Chapter Eight

Holt's phone rang as he was pulling up in front of Sarah's house. The sheriff.

"Did you get the warrant?" Holt asked.

"Yeah, I got it, but neither me nor the judge is overly happy about it. I'm hoping my mother doesn't hear about this until I'm out of my cast and can run fast enough to escape her mouth. She put up a lot of money to get me elected and wouldn't appreciate having made a bad investment if this whole thing goes bad."

"I understand." Holt had heard enough of Lorraine's mouth that afternoon to last a lifetime. Still, he was happy he'd walked up when he did or he had a feeling he would have been serving Alex supper down at town lockup. "What does the warrant cover?"

"The right to search all areas of the island including structures."

"No restrictions?" Holt was a bit surprised that his uncle had gotten that much latitude.

"I specifically asked for no restrictions. I want you at that island at daybreak and done with this wild goose chase by tomorrow night. Then I don't want to hear another weird theory from crazy Sarah again. This parish has enough problems with reputation without crazy women adding to the mix. After tomorrow, you spend your time looking for Bobby Rhonaldo. Is that clear?"

"Yeah, there may be a problem with that." He told his uncle about the pawn shop and Bobby's guitar.

His uncle swore. "Why didn't you tell me about this as soon as you found out? I could have gotten a picture off that video and already had it running in the national database."

"Already taken care of. You're on leave."

"Just how did you manage that when I didn't leave you passwords or instructions for any of those systems?"

"I called in a favor with Max."

"Oh, yeah. That half brother of yours. Well, next time I want you to invite the Baton Rogue Police Department into my investigation, I'll tell you. Is that clear?"

"No problem."

"So what are you doing now?"

"Officially, I'm off the clock, so I don't have to answer that."

"Which means it's something I wouldn't like. Do us all a favor, Holt. Don't create a bunch of problems in this town and then leave again like you did last time. Vodoun's a nice place. I'd like for it to stay that way."

Holt disconnected the call and slipped the phone back in his jeans pocket. A nice town with more disappearing children per capita than any other town in the state. A parish with a reputation so creepy that vendors would deliver to the businesses located within it during only daylight hours. Not the place he'd choose to settle down given that statistic, *if* he were ever inclined to settle down in the first place.

He looked over at Sarah's cute white cottage with blue trim and pretty fall flowers and sighed. He was about to prepare dinner for his ex-girlfriend, when he'd gone halfway around the world to forget, and the mother of the missing child. Yeah, that wasn't even remotely domestic.

Before he changed his mind and drove away, he pushed open the door and stepped out onto the curb. He saw the curtains flutter on the front window and knew someone had peeked outside and seen him. Too late to flee now. At least too late to flee without looking like a coward. Again.

He was going to do his small-town duty and

cook a meal for a friend in trouble. Nothing wrong with that. And maybe, if he could get a little too much wine into Alex, she may tell him what happened to her and Sarah on that island years ago. All this time he'd wondered. And the fact that Alex and Sarah had held to their pact to never tell anyone what had happened let him know it was something serious. Something neither of them wanted to bring back to the forefront of their memory.

He strode up the sidewalk and Alex opened the front door as he approached.

"I thought you were going to change your mind for a minute there," Alex commented.

Because that was exactly what he'd been thinking of doing, he was silent for a second, then finally said, "No, just thinking about a phone call."

"The sheriff?"

"How did you guess?"

"Because your expression wavers between aggravation and looking like you sucked on a lemon. The man does the same thing to me."

Holt laughed. "Well, then I guess I need to get to cooking and improve our moods." Before he stepped in the house, he asked, "How's Sarah doing?"

Alex raised one eyebrow and pointed toward

the kitchen. "Perhaps you should see for yourself."

Holt hesitated for a moment, but when Alex said nothing more, he walked down the hallway to the kitchen, uncertain of what he was going to find. What he saw was the last possible thing he'd expected.

Sarah was standing at the island in her kitchen, hands covered with flour and singing along with a George Strait song playing on the radio. She looked up as he walked into the room and beamed.

"It's about time you made it. I'm getting hungry. And look—I'm making your favorite for dessert—apple pies. I had enough for three so Alex and I will be eating it for a while and you'll be taking one home."

Holt forced a smile. "Thanks," he said to Sarah, then leaned toward Alex, who was standing beside him in the doorway and asked in a low voice, "What did you give her?"

"Oh, doctors can't dispense the sort of drugs that produce those results."

"Then what?"

"Sarah had an appointment with Madam Fredericks this afternoon."

Holt held in a groan. The last thing he needed was that crazy woman getting Sarah's hopes up.

"I see you're as happy about the turn of events as I am," Alex observed.

"What did she say?"

"That Erika would be returned to Sarah."

Holt narrowed his eyes. "But no reference to Erika being alive?"

"Funny how you caught that, too. Seems Sarah's the only one who hasn't."

"Great." Holt sighed. "So what are we supposed to do now?"

"We pretend everything's going to be fine until Sarah goes to bed, then we discuss a plan for tomorrow. Can I assume since your disgruntled uncle called, you got a search warrant?"

"Oh, yeah, much to the dismay of everyone involved except you and I."

Sarah waved a floured hand at the two of them. "What are you guys waiting for? Get started on supper before we starve."

"I guess that's my cue," Holt said. "What kind of tomatoes did you buy?"

Sarah laughed. "Any kind you want." She pointed to the counter behind her.

"Don't say a word," Alex said, when he scanned the counter and looked back at her.

"Wasn't going to."

THREE HOURS LATER, Alex pushed back her almost-empty plate of apple pie, unable to eat another bite. "I'm going to pop," she said.

Sarah took a last bite of her apple pie and nodded. "I won't need to eat again for a week."

"I don't know about a week," Holt said, "but food's definitely not going to be a priority for a while."

Sarah pushed her chair back. "Well, I'm going to take a shower and head to bed. Tomorrow could be a big day, and I want to be my best when my baby comes home."

"Sarah, I think—" Alex started.

"Thank you, Holt," Sarah interrupted, "for preparing a great supper." She gave Alex a knowing look. "I'll just leave you two to wrap up the rest of the night."

As soon as Sarah left the kitchen, Holt laughed. "She could have been a little more subtle," he said.

Alex sighed. "Subtlety was never Sarah's strong point."

"Yours, either, if my memory serves correctly."

"I've gotten worse with age."

"Good. That means you should meet my next question with a direct answer."

Alex immediately shifted from open to closed. Whatever Holt had in mind, she was certain she wasn't going to like it.

"I know you told me to never ask," Holt started.

Alex knew immediately what was coming next. "No," she said, shaking her head.

"The information you have may help us find Erika."

"No, it won't." Alex felt a wave of nausea pass over her as her mind shifted for a split second to those years ago. "I promise you, what I saw won't help anyone."

Alex's emotions waged a war inside her head and heart. She knew she could trust Holt with her secrets, but she couldn't trust him with her heart. Baring her soul to him, especially about that particular item, wasn't something she'd come to Vodoun prepared to do. It wasn't something she'd ever thought about doing.

She tried to formulate the words. Tried to find the exact combination that would convince him to leave this alone, but before she could utter the first word, a thud sounded on the roof directly above them.

She jumped out of her chair a second behind Holt, who had already rushed over to the kitchen window and peered out into the darkness before she could even move from her spot.

"Can you see anything?"

"No. It's pitch-black because of the storm, and the rain is still coming down."

"Someone is on the roof. What else would cause such a noise up there? Sarah is careful to keep her trees trimmed away from the roof of the house."

Holt pulled his pistol from his waistband. "Do you have your weapon?"

Alex nodded and hurried to her bedroom to retrieve her gun.

"Stay here," Holt directed when she returned to the kitchen, "and do not be afraid to use that if anyone but me walks back in this door."

Alex gripped the pistol and watched as Holt unlocked the back door and slipped out onto the porch. A second thud sounded directly above her, and she clenched the pistol tighter.

"What's going on? I heard a noise on the roof." Sarah rushed into the kitchen, her hair still wet from the shower and her eyes wide. "Oh, my God. What are you doing with a gun?"

"We heard the noise, and Holt has gone outside to investigate. Just stay behind me."

At the sound of rustling on the porch, Alex directed her attention back to the door. What was Holt doing out there? What had he found?

She knew he'd told her to wait, but what if he needed help? He'd had enough time to investigate if it was something innocuous.

"Stay here," she told Sarah, and crept up to the back door. She edged the door open a crack and peered outside in the darkness.

Holt stood at the edge of the porch, staring

down at the ground. His pistol was back in his waistband, so Alex assumed no threat existed for the moment. She slipped out the back door and walked up beside him to see what had captured his interest. When she looked at the flower bed that surrounded the porch, she gasped.

A dead crow lay in the midst of Sarah's fall flowers.

When Alex gasped, Holt whirled around. "I told you to stay inside," he said.

"I thought you might need help."

"I do. I need help explaining what the hell is going on here." He waved one hand out at the yard, and Alex raised her gaze beyond the flower bed.

The porch light didn't reach very far into the backyard, but its reach was beyond the carefully groomed flower beds. Alex could see the dark shadows lying at random on the lawn. All about the same size. The size of a crow.

"We can't let Sarah see this," Alex said.

"Let me see what?" Sarah's voice sounded from the doorway.

Alex whirled around, but Sarah had already stepped out onto the porch, her attention drawn to a black patch off the back of the porch. Before Alex could stop her, she leaned over and let out a cry.

Alex rushed to her and placed her arm around Sarah's shoulder, pulling her back in the house. Holt followed behind and closed the door behind them.

Sarah began to wail as soon as they stopped in the kitchen. "It's an omen. You saw it. Madam Fredericks lied. She said my baby was going to come back to me, but the dead crows can only mean one thing."

All of a sudden, Sarah froze and stared at Alex, her eyes wide. "She didn't say Erika would come back alive," she whispered.

All the color washed from Sarah's face, and Alex moved forward to catch her just as she slumped to the floor. As Alex's knees buckled, Holt caught Sarah and lifted her up in his arms.

"Her bedroom," Alex said, and pointed Holt down the hall.

He placed Sarah on her bed and Alex gave her cousin a check. "Her vital signs are fine," Alex said. "She'll probably come out of it in a minute."

"Maybe it would be better if she didn't."

Alex bit her lower lip. "Even if it was legal, I can't keep her drugged until we find Erika."

Holt sighed. "I know. And I wasn't suggesting you do that. I just wish she didn't have to suffer this much." He ran one hand through his hair. "I can't imagine what she must be feeling."

"I can't, either," Alex replied, a bit surprised that Holt had even thought about the depth of Sarah's feelings, much less voiced his thoughts. His time away from Vodoun had changed him, and in a good way. He was more conscientious. More aware.

More attractive.

She shook her head to clear her thoughts. Not wanting to think about how with every thoughtful action, her heart opened back up to Holt just a bit. Not wanting to think about how she was going to feel when this was all over and she was back to her normal life in New Orleans. It was too much on top of everything else she was dealing with.

As if reading her thoughts, Holt moved next to her and placed his arm around her.

"We're going to figure this out. I promise you."

Alex nodded and tried not to think about how good his arm felt around her. There was a time when all Alex needed was Holt's touch to be certain that everything was going to be right in her world. She wanted desperately to believe that again.

THE KILLER WATCHED THE house from behind a hedge across the street. He'd seen the fake sheriff enter earlier, and he was still there. The three of them stuck together, just as his boss had warned they would. Which could easily become a problem.

Apparently, the shots his associate had fired at them had deterred them from returning to the island, unless it was the weather that was keeping them away. He'd know by tomorrow which it was, as the storm was due to break early in the morning.

The killer had thought all the smokescreen and mirrors with the doll was unnecessary fluff added to a simple kidnapping, but as suspicion had immediately fallen to the witch woman, he had to admit that perhaps his boss had been right. The past might well be enough to permanently divert suspicion, especially in Mystere Parish, where people expected the out-of-the-ordinary.

He had no idea why his boss had him kidnap the girl, nor what was planned for the child in the future, and that puzzled him. In the time he'd known the boss, the only focus had been on making money. He had no idea where a missing six-year-old fit into building a financial empire.

And he wasn't about to ask.

The boss called the shots and wrote the checks. His job was not to question but to perform.

He left the hedge and stepped into his car,

which he'd parked around the corner. Tomorrow, he'd see whether or not they returned to the island. Then he'd report to his boss and discuss further action needed.

THE PIERCING SOUND of his alarm woke Holt only seconds before his cell phone rang. He glanced at the clock and groaned. Five a.m. A mere three hours after he'd finally crawled into bed after a long night helping Alex get Sarah to a semblance of calm.

He reached for his cell phone as he rose from the bed. His pulse quickened a bit when he saw the number for the laboratory that was testing the barrette.

"Chamberlain," he answered.

"Mr. Chamberlain," the lab tech said, "we were able to lift three fingerprints off the barrette you gave us. Two of them got hits in the system."

"Tell me."

"The first hit was for Sarah Rhonaldo."

Holt felt his pulse quicken. The barrette had belonged to Erika. "And the second?"

"Mathilde Tregre."

"Thanks for getting this done so quickly," Holt said.

"Anything to help," the tech said. "We're all hoping you find that little girl alive."

"Me, too." Holt tossed the cell phone onto the bed and grabbed a pair of jeans and a T-shirt from the closet. Time to grab a quick bite to eat and get to the dock to meet Alex.

Last night, he'd tried to convince her to stay with Sarah today instead of returning to the island. He'd told her he'd get the deputy to help him, but Vodoun was a small town, and Alex already knew the deputy had just left on vacation and wasn't returning for a week. She'd thanked him for the offer but assured him she'd feel better looking for answers rather than being cooped up in Sarah's house. She had a nurse friend from New Orleans coming to sit with her cousin for the day, and she insisted there was no point in arguing.

And that was that.

Alex was already pacing the dock when he arrived. The dark circles under her eyes gave away her long night. He handed her a large cup of coffee he'd picked up at the gas station along the way and she gave him a small smile.

"I didn't even remember to bring any," she said.

"How's Sarah?"

"Calm now, but I'm afraid the slightest thing could send her right back to hysterical. My friend arrived an hour ago, so she'll be fine."

"Good, because I need you to concentrate on

the job ahead of us. With the sky still overcast from the rain, it's going to make visibility dim."

"Then I guess we best get going."

Alex started to step into the boat, but Holt placed his hand on her arm to stop her. "There's something else."

He told her about the lab results on the barrette. Her eyes widened and she covered her mouth with her hand.

"The witch woman has her. Just like Sarah said. But where?"

"We don't know anything for certain," he cautioned, "except that Erika's barrette was on the island and Mathilde Tregre had it. We don't know for sure if Erika was ever there or Mathilde brought the barrette from somewhere else."

"We're going to find out," she said, her jaw set.

Chapter Nine

Holt pushed the boat away from the dock and studied Alex as he guided the boat across the bayou. She looked straight ahead, her body rigid. The two times she'd glanced back at him, she wore a determined look. He gripped the steering wheel of the boat tighter, frustrated that he was unable to do more to alleviate her stress. Frustrated that he couldn't fix this problem for her and Sarah like he had others when they were kids.

The ride to the island was rougher than the last time they'd gone, the bayou waters choppy from the wind rushing across it. Still, it seemed to Holt that they got to the island quicker. Of course, he knew exactly where they were going this time.

As they approached the island dock, he cut the boat's speed and crept slowly toward the bank, scanning the brush for any signs of the shooter. He was there with a warrant, but if someone shot first and asked questions later, he and Alex could be on the losing end. The swamp was quiet, the top of the water barely glistening from the slivers of sun breaking through the clouds.

He guided the boat to the dock and eased the nose of it onto shore. Frowning, he scanned the area around them one more time before cutting power to the engine. Holt would never admit it to anyone, but the dolls were sort of unnerving. For whatever reason, the sight of them reminded him of death, and he'd seen far too much of that overseas.

Alex looked back at him as the engine wound down. "I didn't see anything," she said.

"Me, either, but that doesn't mean someone's not out there. They could be waiting until we're on land and easier to pick off, especially since we got away the last time."

"There's a comforting thought."

"Sorry, but I need you to be alert and ready for anything. If you're on edge, you have an advantage."

Alex nodded. "So do we head to the cabin?"

"Yeah. I have a copy of the warrant. If Mathilde Tregre is there, I can present her with it. If not, I plan on leaving a copy tacked to the door. Maybe if she knows we have the right to be here, she won't shoot at us."

"Assuming it's her that took the shots in the first place."

"Exactly. We're dealing with a bunch of unknowns here. Are you ready?"

Alex glanced at the dolls surrounding the dock. "As ready as I'm getting."

"I'll take the lead, but follow closely, and keep your gun ready."

Holt stepped past Alex and onto the bank, then reached back to offer her his hand getting out of the boat. As soon as both her feet hit ground, he headed down the trail that they'd taken before to the cabin.

They moved slower than he would have liked to, but moving faster made it harder to listen for other creatures, especially the careful, bipedal kind. The path showed no sign of recent passage, but any footprints left the night before would have been washed away in the storm. And whoever shot at them might have taken a completely different route to the dock. There was no telling how many paths and trails were carved through the island. The old woman and her ancestors had occupied the island for over a hundred years. Plenty of time to create multiple paths, both for hunting and being hunted.

As they closed in on the cabin's clearing, he stopped and peered out of the foliage, looking for any sign of life in the tiny structure. The swamp was eerily quiet, as if every living creature were holding its breath, just waiting for his next move. Finally, he motioned to Alex to stay put and crept out of the brush to the side of the cabin. Once safely pressed against the structure, he waved at Alex to join him, then eased along the side of the cabin and around the corner to the front door.

The door was still unlocked as he'd left it. He peered around the corner, but the cabin was empty. Broken glass crunched beneath his feet as he stepped inside. He studied the cabin for a minute, then looked over at Alex, who was standing silently beside him.

"Doesn't look like anything's been moved," he said.

"No. You'd think if she'd been back here, she would have at least cleaned up the glass in the doorway."

"You'd think," Holt agreed.

Alex bit her lower lip. "So what now?"

Holt blew out a breath. "I guess we start poking through the brush like we did yesterday. There's no rain in the forecast today, so at least we have that on our side."

"How big is this island?"

"About ten square miles, give or take for erosion."

Alex shook her head. "There's no way we

can cover that in a day—not every inch. And if the woman has Erika, she can easily move her away from whatever area we're searching. She's got the advantage here. In a big way."

"Yeah," Holt agreed. "But we don't have another option. The trail we were on the other day didn't seem to be well used. Let's try around behind the cabin and see if we can find another entry point there."

Holt pulled the copy of the warrant from his wallet and pushed it over a nail in the center of the front door on their way out. A fairly defined trail started behind the cabin, almost in the center of the clearing, so they started down it.

"No footprints," Holt noted. "No one's passed here since the storm."

"Do you think she could have another cabin on the island?"

"Could be multiple cabins. Even if she did minimal maintenance, they would offer her places to escape the storm or different starting locations for hunting and fishing."

"And herb gathering. Most of those jars in the cabin had roots and dried plants in them."

"Yeah," he acknowledged, but didn't say more. He still didn't know what to think about the woman and her glass jar collection. He knew people still believed and practiced the old ways, and Mathilde Tregre would be a prime candidate given her family history on the island and reclusive tendencies. But he deliberately kept that line of thinking from his investigation because he didn't want to think about the other side of it—did it work?

They progressed slowly through the swamp for about an hour before reaching the shore on the opposite side. Holt looked across the channel into the swamp, but there was no sign of life anywhere near. The trail hadn't contained any forks along the way, so clearly it was intended to reach this bank.

"Maybe she uses it to reach this side for fishing," Holt suggested.

"The distance across the island is shorter than the length, right?" Alex wiped her brow with the back of her hand. "Maybe we should try to walk alongside the bank for a bit and see if we find anything."

Holt nodded. "Let's try the right side first. It doesn't look as dense."

But before he took a single step, a scream rang out through the swamp. Alex clenched his arm with both hands and stared at him, wide-eyed.

Holt pointed to the right and whispered, "It sounds like it came from that direction." He checked his pistol and motioned for Alex to follow him.

They crept through the brush along the bank, listening for movement, but the swamp had gone quiet again. Suddenly, Alex stopped short and tugged on his sleeve. She pointed to the brush ahead of them. Holt stood still and finally he heard the faint sound of weeping. All thought for safety aside, he rushed through the brush in the direction of the crying. He burst through a hedge of dense brush and found himself face-to-face with a twelve-foot alligator.

"Stay back," he yelled at Alex, but it was already too late. As she slid to a stop beside him, the alligator swung its enormous head toward them.

That's when Holt saw that it had something bloody clasped in its jaws. He sucked in a breath when he realized it was a human leg. He heard Alex stifle a cry and knew she'd seen it, as well.

The alligator hissed, his gaze locked on Alex.

"Can you shoot him?" she whispered.

"Too close, and if I miss…" He didn't have to finish his sentence. Alex had grown up in the swamp and knew the odds as well as he did.

"We passed a cypress tree about twenty feet back," she said.

He nodded, but didn't take his eye off the alligator. He saw the animal's front leg quiver and a wave of fear washed over him. If the animal rose up on his legs, he would strike. Even a beast that large could move much faster than a human.

The alligator's gaze was fixed on Alex. He hissed again and began to lift up his body to strike.

"Go!" Holt jumped in front of Alex and pushed her back toward the tree.

The alligator leaped forward, and he spun to the right, barely dodging the razor-sharp teeth of the beast. He knew he had only seconds to get away before the alligator managed to swing his body around and launch at him again. Praying that Alex was safely off the ground, he spun around again and bolted for the tree.

He heard the marsh grass crunching as the alligator threw his entire length forward through the brush. Every muscle in his body strained as he pushed his body to the limit to cover the distance to the tree before the alligator closed the gap to him. It was only twenty feet, but seemed much farther before he leaped in the air and grabbed the lowest branch of the cypress tree, dropping his pistol as he went. He felt a tug on his jeans and heard the material rip as he pulled himself up into the tree, narrowly escaping the deadly jaws of the alligator.

He swung his leg over the branch and leaned back against the trunk of the tree in a sitting position. "That was close," he said.

"Too close."

One look at Alex's face told him just how close it had been. All the color had washed completely from her face. Her eyes were wide as saucers and she picked involuntarily at the branch she clung to.

"Are you sure he didn't get you?" she asked, her voice cracking.

"Just the end of my jeans." He couldn't remember the last time he'd felt so close to death. Even the shooter from the other night hadn't sent him into overdrive the way the alligator had.

"What are we going to do?"

"I'm going to fire a warning shot," Holt said. "See if I can scare him off. But I'll need your pistol. I dropped mine when I jumped into the tree."

"Even if you scare him off, that doesn't mean he won't come back. He's fast, Holt. Faster than I've ever seen before."

"I'm well aware of that, but I can't make a kill shot from this angle, and we can't sit in this tree waiting for him to die." Holt moved sideways on the branch a bit to give himself a better view of the alligator.

"Hand me your gun," he said, and Alex passed him her pistol.

He aimed at the ground just to the side of the alligator and fired a single bullet. The instant the bullet struck the ground, the alligator whirled around and scurried through the brush. A huge splash followed seconds later.

"Do you think that belongs to the person who screamed?" Alex pointed to what was left of the leg that the alligator had left in front of the tree.

Holt gave a mental sigh of relief as he gave the leg a closer look and determined it belonged to an adult and not a child.

"We need to find out," he said. "They may need help."

"If that's their leg, it's too late to help."

"They might not be alone."

Alex nodded and Holt dropped out of the tree and onto the ground. He tucked the pistol in his waistband and reached up to assist Alex in climbing out of the tree. Once she was safely on the ground behind him, he edged through the brush back toward the clearing where they'd encountered the alligator.

The brush across the clearing showed signs of passage. Branches were broken off shrubs and the marsh grass was flattened. Holt studied the bank, looking for any sign of their man-eating friend, but he couldn't see any bubbles on the water, a telltale sign that an alligator was resting below the surface. He hurried across the clearing, Alex close behind, and followed the trail of broken branches deeper into the swamp.

He almost tripped over the woman who was lying in a bunch of marsh grass. She was old, and her long silver hair stuck out in every direction. He felt a rush of relief pass over him as he noted both legs were intact. But the woman was injured. Her arm was covered in blood and she wasn't responsive when he called out.

Alex gasped when she peered around him, but then she pushed past him and dropped to the ground, her medical training taking over. "Her pulse is strong," she said.

"Did she pass out from blood loss?"

Alex shook her head. "Not unless she lost a lot more than what we see here. Likely, it was fright and stress and age." She looked up at Holt. "She's the witch woman."

"Mathilde Tregre. I figured."

The woman stirred and then her eyes popped open. She stared at Alex and then tried to push herself up.

"Wait," Alex said, holding her shoulders.

"You've been injured. I need to tie off your arm and get the bleeding to stop."

The woman's eyes flashed from Alex to Holt, her fear evident.

"I'm a doctor," Alex said. "Do you understand?"

"The gator?" the woman asked.

"Gone," Holt said.

"He had a piece…a leg it looked like," she said. "I was on him before I realized it. He got a bite of my hand, but I managed to pull away before he could clamp down."

"You're lucky," Alex said. She removed her belt and placed it around the woman's arm.

"Are you Mathilde Tregre?" Holt asked.

The old woman winced as Alex tightened the belt on her arm. "I'm Mathilde. I hope you weren't here looking for the rest of whoever that alligator had in his mouth."

"No. We're looking for a little girl."

Mathilde jerked her head up to stare at Holt. "And you figured the witch woman must have taken her."

"We found a pink barrette in your cabin yesterday," Alex said. "It belonged to the little girl who's missing."

Mathilde studied Alex for a moment. "Is it your little girl?"

"She's my cousin's daughter."

"I don't know where she is."

"But you have the barrette."

"I was saving it. For the full moon."

"You were going to do a reading?" Alex asked.

Mathilde nodded. "Ain't no kids been on this island since I was a kid. Ain't none belongs here. It's a dangerous place, but it's my place."

"Ms. Tregre," Holt said. "I need to ask you some questions, but it's more important that we get some medical attention for your hand."

"Am I under arrest?"

"If that's what it takes to get you to the hospital, then yes."

"I ain't got nothing to hide. Didn't all them years ago and don't now. 'Course that won't stop the lies, will it?"

"I'm only interested in the truth," Holt assured her.

"Then you'd be the only one."

"Can you make it back to your cabin?" Holt asked. "I can go back and bring the boat around, but that will take longer."

"I'm fine to walk," Mathilde said. "Probably in better shape than either one of you."

Holt looked up at Alex, who nodded.

Satisfied that Mathilde was healthy enough to make the trek, he helped Alex lift her to a standing position.

"If you feel dizzy," Alex instructed, "let me know and we'll rest."

"Stop your fussing," Mathilde said. "I'll be fine."

Alex looked over at him. "Should we... I mean, we ought to...the leg."

The leg.

He needed to get what was left of it back to Vodoun. There was always the slim chance that it contained some identifiable characteristic.

"Yeah, I'll just..." The last thing he wanted to do was carry the thing with his hands.

"Here," Alex said and pulled off her T-shirt, exposing the tank she wore beneath it. "Wrap it in that as best you can."

Holt returned to the bank and secured what was left of the leg as well as he could, then returned to Mathilde and Alex.

"Let's go," he said.

The trip back to the dock took longer than Holt would have liked, but actually went faster than he expected. Mathilde hadn't overstated her claims of physical fitness. The old woman moved at a good clip through the swamp and never once asked for a break. He couldn't help but think they could have used someone with her fortitude in his troop in Iraq.

A million questions rushed through his mind, but he managed to keep them all in. Talking would have slowed them down and winded

Mathilde. The sooner they got to the hospital in New Orleans and got her medical care, the sooner he could cover everything that needed covering.

Chapter Ten

"How is she?" Alex asked the doctor as he stepped out of the room.

"The alligator clipped her good on her hand," the doctor said, "but missed the nerves. She was lucky."

"And otherwise?"

"Oh, she's healthy as a horse, especially for her age. I guess there's something to be said for living off the land."

"And her mental faculties?"

The doctor smiled. "Now, that would be your area, not mine, but if you want my opinion, I think she's alert, focused and completely sane."

Alex let out a breath of relief. "Thanks."

"Can I question her?" Holt asked.

The doctor frowned. "Of course, she's healthy enough to be questioned, but what crime is involved with being attacked by an alligator?"

"That alligator had a human leg in his mouth,"

Holt said, "and there's a missing girl that we have reason to believe was on the island."

"Wow," the doctor said. "Well, then please go about your business. I hope you find the missing girl." He gave Alex a nod and left.

Alex and Holt entered the room, where Mathilde sat propped up in a hospital bed, her bandaged hand clutching a television remote that she held above her head, as if the height would make it function better. Alex froze for a moment and a wave of fear washed over her. With her arm in the air and her silver hair loose and awry, it flashed Alex right back to that day. That day she and Sarah saw something that wasn't possible.

She took a deep breath to calm her racing heart and stepped up to the bed.

"Can't get this thing to stop making noise," Mathilde complained, pressing the buttons on the remote. "A person can't think with all that racket."

Alex took the remote from her and turned off the television. Mathilde slumped back on the bed. "Thanks," she said.

"How do you feel?" Alex asked.

"I'm fine. All this fussing about, trying to give me that poison in a bottle. Told the woman I just need my herbs. Young folk don't know anything these days."

"Ms. Tregre," Holt began, "you may not be able to return to your island for a while. If you're in pain, the medicine can help. I assure you, it's not poison."

"Says you. And what do you mean, I can't return to my island? You said earlier I wasn't under arrest."

"No, but I do need to ask you some questions, and your answers coupled with other facts will dictate how I move forward. Can you answer questions now?"

"Of course. I'm talking, aren't I? Get on with it so I can get back to my quiet life. Too many people here. Always talking. I like silence."

Alex dug into her purse and pulled out her tape recorder that she was never without. "You can use this."

Holt pressed Record and began. "Let's start with the alligator. He had the remains of a human leg in his mouth when we came across him. Do you have any idea who that person could be?"

"No. Ain't nobody lives on that island but me, and ain't nobody supposed to be there but me."

"Did you see or hear the alligator attack the man?"

"No. I was walking the shoreline, checking

my fishing lines, and was on him before I knew it. He got my hand before I could get away."

"Was the person there when you came upon the gator?"

"Just the piece you saw."

"Do you have any idea what time that was?"

Mathilde snorted. "Don't have no use for time. When it's dark, I sleep. When it's light, I work."

"Do you have any idea how long you were lying there before we found you?"

"About as long as it takes to cook a meal and eat, I suppose. However long that is."

"Maybe an hour," Alex suggested.

"What difference does it make what time it was?" Mathilde asked. "The only thing left was the leg, and the man shouldn't have been there to begin with."

"The little girl that we're looking for...her father is also missing."

Mathilde sighed. "That's not good. Do you think he brought the girl to the island? Why would he do that? The island's mine, but even if it wasn't, it's no place for city people."

"You said you found the barrette. Can you tell us when you found it and where?"

Mathilde nodded. "Day before yesterday. It was on the bank around near where the alligator was today."

"But you saw no other signs that anyone had been on the island?"

"Wasn't any footprints, and the marsh grass didn't show any sign that someone had docked a boat along that bank."

Holt looked over at Alex who gave him a slight nod. As far as she could tell, the woman was being truthful.

"Ms. Tregre," Holt continued. "We visited the island two days ago and when we were leaving, someone tried to shoot us. Was that you?"

"Of course not! You think I'd waste bullets on people? There's a lot more dangerous things on that island than people."

"Maybe not," Holt said.

Mathilde scrunched her brow and stared at the wall behind him for a couple of seconds, then nodded. "Maybe not anymore."

Holt sighed. "That's all the questions I have for you, Ms. Tregre. When the doctor releases you, I'll be glad to take you back to the island, but I'll have to ask you not to leave the state until my investigation is complete."

"Ha." Mathilde snorted. "Wouldna left the island excepting you made me."

Alex stared at Mathilde, questions burning in her mind. Questions she knew Holt wouldn't appreciate and questions that normally would have been the last thing on her mind. But she knew if she didn't ask, she'd regret it.

"Ms. Tregre," Alex began, "you said you were going to use the barrette to do a reading. What would that tell you?"

"Whether the owner of the barrette was alive, for one. And if she was on the island, I might get a direction from the smoke. It's hard to tell as the farther away they are, the harder the reading."

"Do you think you can still do that?"

"'Course. Assuming I'm back on the island. Ain't gonna work from this bed. Full moon starts tonight. That's what I was waiting for. Lot more power with the full moon."

"There's something else. Something I'm hoping you can explain."

"I can try."

She told Mathilde about the crows that had fallen onto Sarah's house and yard. Mathilde's eyes widened and she started shaking her head before Alex finished telling the story.

"Did they fall in other yards or just your cousin's?" Mathilde asked.

"Just Sarah's."

"And she's the mama of the missing girl?"

"Yes."

"That's not good. And the crow was watching the girl before she disappeared, you said?"

Alex nodded. Mathilde stared down at her blanket and picked at a loose thread with her fingers. Alex could tell she knew something but didn't want to say.

"What does it mean?" Alex asked. "Is it an omen?"

Mathilde took a deep breath and blew it out, then looked up at Alex. "No. It's a curse."

HOLT PLACED HIS HAND on Alex's arm to steady her as they left Mathilde's room. Mathilde's words had shaken her, and despite his refusal to believe there was anything going on here but a very real crime committed by very real people, he had to admit the woman was kinda spooky.

"She's telling the truth," Alex said, her voice shaky.

"I agree," Holt said, "but is her truth our reality?"

"Ah, you've just hit on the most difficult part of my job. Yes, it's possible that someone can absolutely believe what they're saying even if it's not true."

"And do you get that from her?"

Alex frowned. "It's too hard to say with minimal contact. Mathilde's a recluse and practices the old ways. Those two aspects already put her outside of normal, and you'd have to exclude any behaviors due to those in order to get to the root of her mind."

Holt sighed. "So we don't know any more now than we did before. Not for certain."

"I'm inclined to lean toward believing her statements as factual unless they're proven otherwise. *And* we have the leg."

"Which isn't going to do us a bit of good unless the person's DNA is in the system."

"There's still a chance. I had the nurse pack it for us."

"Good. We can take it to the lab. See what they can find."

Alex nodded and walked down the hall toward the exit. Holt watched her for a couple of seconds, wondering what had stopped her cold the moment they'd stepped into the old woman's room. It must be something to do with what she and Sarah had seen on the island when they were kids. The old woman unnerved Alex, and that was something he'd never seen before.

Sooner or later, she was going to have to face whatever she'd tucked away, because it seemed as if it was coming full circle. The same way his past was for him.

HOLT HANDED THE LAB TECH the container with the leg and explained the situation. The tech's eyes widened as Holt described the condition of the body part and how they came by it.

"I'll get right on this," the tech said. "Just fill out the forms at the front desk and leave me a phone number where I can reach you."

Holt nodded, and the tech left the front office with the container. The administrative assistant at the front desk handed him the paperwork, a clipboard and a pen, and he moved to some chairs at the back of the room to enter the necessary information.

"How long will it take?" Alex asked.

"Days, probably. They have to take a sample and type the DNA, then run it through the system."

"So not like on TV?"

"Not even close."

Holt completed the forms and returned them to the front desk. He pulled a card with his contact information on it out and handed it to the administrative assistant. "Can you please attach that to the paperwork? It has all my contact numbers on there. I'd like to know something as soon as you do."

"Of course," the woman said and stapled the card to the top of the paperwork. "I think that's all we need for now. We'll be in touch as soon as the lab finishes their work."

"Thank you," he said, and they made their way to the front door.

Before they stepped outside, the door to the secure area of the building flew open and the lab tech hurried into the waiting room. He looked excited when he saw them standing there.

"Good, I caught you," he said.

"You found something so quickly?" Holt asked.

"This is one of those rare instances where we can identify the body part with absolute certainty. The leg had a pin in it with a serial number."

"And you can track the person by that serial number?" Holt asked.

"Absolutely. A simple phone call and I have your John Doe identified as one Mr. Bobby Rhonaldo."

Alex sucked in a breath and felt a wave of dizziness pass over her. Holt placed one arm around her shoulders and guided her to a chair. She bent over, drawing in a deep breath, then rose back to a sitting position.

"I'm sorry," she said. "I knew it was possible. I thought I was prepared."

"Mr. Rhonaldo is her cousin by marriage," Holt explained to the anxious tech.

"I'm very sorry," the tech said.

"I hate to have to ask you this," Holt said, "because I know the leg is in bad condition and the handling hasn't been all that great on my end, either. But can you check to see if there's evidence of any other person?"

"What do you mean?"

"Mr. Rhonaldo's six-year-old daughter is also missing. I'm hoping she wasn't with Mr. Rhonaldo."

The tech's eye widened. "Oh, no. Of course, I'll do what I can, but it will take a while."

Holt nodded. "Her DNA is already in the system—Erika Rhonaldo. Whatever you can do, I'd appreciate."

THE KILLER WATCHED AS THE cop and the doctor left the lab. He'd followed them as they took the old woman to New Orleans and hidden in a linen closet across from the old lady's room. He'd heard their entire conversation after they'd interviewed the woman.

If only they'd arrived on the island ten minutes later. The alligator would have finished the job. The old woman had ruined it all by interrupting the beast while he was having a snack. Of course, there was also the small issue of why his associate had chosen that location in the swamp to dispose of the body. Something he'd failed to mention when he reported shooting at the fake sheriff and the woman the first time they visited the island.

The associate was only supposed to place the barrette on the island so that they could further incriminate the old woman. Apparently, he thought he'd combine two jobs into one, and now his laziness was about to upset the entire mix.

If Bobby Rhonaldo's DNA was in the system, the lab could identify who the leg belonged to. Then everyone would know for certain that Bobby Rhonaldo hadn't left the country with his daughter, which was unfortunate. His boss's idea to stage things to also implicate the old woman had been a good one, but he wondered if it would be enough.

With Bobby's body found on the island, even more evidence pointed toward the old woman. It was all circumstantial, but even the woman shrink wasn't convinced the old woman was sane. All the rumor and uncertainty coupled with the past would play right into convicting the old woman in everyone's mind, if not in court. Still, it would be even better for him and his boss if that leg was not identified.

Was Bobby Rhonaldo's DNA in the system? That was the question.

He pulled his car into the alley behind the lab. Best he retrieve the leg before the tech ran tests. Cutting off that avenue of investigation would keep suspicion on Bobby.

His boss believed that with the girl gone, Vodoun would finally revert back to the unspoiled place it had once been. The killer didn't pretend to understand his boss's motivations, but he was ready to get back to normal. According to his boss, in a couple of weeks, everything would be perfect.

And perfect sounded quite nice.

HOLT STOOD IN FRONT OF the lab, next to the truck, and looked over at Alex. "I guess we should get back to Vodoun," he said, feeling somewhat at a loss. They'd covered a lot of ground since that morning but seemed no closer to finding Erika than they were before. All he'd managed was more unanswered questions, except for locating Bobby Rhonaldo, and that was hardly the answer Holt had wanted.

Alex looked as miserable with the situation as he was, but he couldn't help but admire her strength and focus when most people would have fallen apart. She probably had no idea how attractive that strength and loyalty made her, but Holt hadn't missed a thing. The girl who'd impressed him so much with her focus and determination had become an admirable woman.

She stared down the street at nothing in particular, frowning. Finally, she said, "I should check on Sarah."

Holt nodded, and they climbed into the truck. "Let's get a bite to eat before we head back. It's been a long morning."

"I'm really not hungry at all."

"Neither am I, but we both need to eat."

Alex sighed, but didn't argue. He was right and she knew it.

"There's a deli a couple of blocks over. A cup of soup and a sandwich shouldn't be too hard to manage."

Alex nodded, so he started the truck and pulled away from the curb.

They needed to eat. That was the truth, but Holt knew the real reason he'd suggested sitting in a restaurant rather than taking the sandwiches to go was because he was stalling. For what, he had no idea. Maybe because given everything that had happened so far that day, he felt he needed more to go back to Vodoun with. But what, he had no idea.

He'd exhausted his line of questioning with Mathilde Tregre, and neither he nor Alex thought the woman was being untruthful, at least not to her own knowledge. It might take hours for the tech to find anything on the leg or a day or more to determine there was noth-

ing to find. There was no use in waiting around
New Orleans for that.

But something kept him from guiding his
truck onto the service road and heading south.

They each ordered soup and a sandwich and
took a seat at a vacant table in the far corner
of the café, away from the other patrons. Alex
took one sip of her soup, then dropped the
spoon in her bowl.

"We're cowards," she said.

Holt stared at her.

"We're sitting here eating lunch because neither one of us wants to go back to Vodoun and
tell Sarah that Bobby's dead and we still have
no idea where Erika is."

He frowned. That statement was a little too
close to the truth for comfort, although he
hadn't admitted it to himself until now.

"I prefer to think of it as we're taking time
to decide on the best way to present this new
information," he said.

"By sitting silently in a deli?"

Holt sighed. "What do you want me to say?
I know this looks bad. Really bad."

He stared out the café window for a couple of seconds then looked back at Alex. "Do
you think Sarah's going to be that upset over
Bobby? I mean, they *were* getting a divorce."

"Bobby's affair didn't make Sarah stop loving him. She just couldn't trust him any longer, and without trust, she felt there was no marriage. Time is the only thing that will erase her love for him, and it's only been a couple of months."

He took a bite of his sandwich and rolled that one around in his mind. He'd known Sarah would be upset about Bobby's death, but he'd thought of it in relation to Erika. Not once had he considered that Sarah might still love Bobby, but he guessed it made sense. God knows, he'd seen his mother and Lorraine struggle with their cheating spouses—a father-and-son duo who seemed to delight in leaving unhappy women in their wakes.

His mother had cut her cheating spouse loose when his mistress came up pregnant within months of her own pregnancy with Holt, but they'd "reconciled" more times than he could remember, despite the fact that his father had gone on to father two sons with two different women. Lorraine, on the other hand, had chosen to stay married and spend the rest of her life punishing her husband for his many indiscretions. Likely, it had been a full-time job.

"So how do we tell her without sending her completely off the deep end?" Holt asked.

Alex shook her head. "I don't know that it's possible at this point. I'm thinking…"

"What? If you have any ideas, I'm all ears."

"No, it's wrong." She stared down at her soup, a guilty expression on her face.

Holt immediately understood. "You don't want to tell her yet."

"It crossed my mind. I mean, what's a day or two, right? Just a bit of time to see if we can find Erika. Finding Erika would make Bobby's loss more tolerable."

"So we don't tell her. You and I are the only people who have to know what the tech found."

"But it's dishonest."

"Not unless she asks and you lie."

Alex frowned. "That's a really fine line you're walking there."

"Life isn't always black and white."

Alex studied him with an expectant look, and he knew she wanted him to elaborate. To talk about the experiences he'd had that had led him to such a conclusion, especially as it was a complete departure from the boy who'd left for the Middle East. The boy who thought there was only black or white and no middle ground.

But Holt wasn't about to talk about the things he'd seen. Wasn't about to try and explain to such a civilized person the atrocities he'd seen. No one deserved to carry such things around with them, but he especially didn't want anyone he cared about having those images in their head.

"So maybe we wait a couple of days," he said finally. "It's for her own good, right?"

"Yeah. Let's just keep telling ourselves that." She took a sip of her soup. "So what now? The doctors will keep Mathilde overnight, so that's done for today. The lab will take a while, and even if they find anything, they can tell you by phone."

Holt considered their limited options, none of which he liked.

"Should we go back to the island?" she asked. "To, you know...look for the rest..."

Holt blew out a breath. "I don't know. The body was probably dumped in the bayou. Killers don't usually like to leave evidence lying around."

"So you think the alligator found it... Bobby...in the bayou somewhere and not on land?"

Holt nodded. "I'll have to search the island, of course. I want everything by the book, but I'd be surprised if we found anything relevant."

"And the barrette?"

"I just don't know, and I'd like to have an educated guess before we talk to Sarah about all this."

"I think—"

Holt's cell phone sounded off, interrupting

Alex. He glanced at the display and was surprised to see it was the lab.

"Holt Chamberlain," he answered.

"Mr. Chamberlain, this is Officer Marceau with the New Orleans Police Department. There's a situation at the laboratory you visited earlier today. Are you in a position to come here and help us make some sense of this?"

"What happened?"

"Someone broke in the back entry and assaulted the technician who was working on your case."

Holt straightened in his seat. "Is he okay?"

"He got a good knock on the head, but he's going to be all right. I'm afraid, though, that the assailant left with your evidence."

"What?"

"I'll explain everything when you arrive. Are you nearby, or have you returned to Vodoun?"

"No. I'm in a deli a couple of blocks away. I'll be there in a minute."

"What's wrong?" Alex asked.

"We have to go," Holt said and filled her in on what the police officer had told him.

"Oh, no!" Alex jumped up from the booth and hurried out of the deli after Holt.

He pulled away from the curb and glanced over at Alex, who was staring out the windshield, her expression a mixture of worry and confusion.

"But how did he know about the leg?" she asked, looking over at him.

Holt clenched the steering wheel. "He must have been following us," Holt replied, knowing it was pointless to try and keep it from her.

Alex's eyes widened. "Since when? The hospital? Vodoun? The island? Surely, you would have noticed a tail."

Holt shook his head, frustrated with his failure. "I didn't notice a tail from Vodoun and certainly not from the island. Gossip spreads fast, though. Someone in Vodoun could have tipped him off that we were transporting Mathilde to the hospital in New Orleans."

"You think there's more than one person involved?"

"Maybe. Or maybe someone passed on the information, not knowing the implications."

"But no one from Vodoun would tell this to anyone that wasn't aware of Mathilde and the island."

"I know."

She sucked in a breath. "It's someone local, isn't it? It always has been."

"Probably."

She turned to stare back out the window, and he knew her mind was reeling from the possibility that she knew the person who'd caused all this heartache for her family. What Holt wasn't about to tell her was even worse—that he suspected the killer wasn't working alone. That more than one person in the community might be working together to cause all this damage.

And that they may have been working in Vodoun long before now.

Chapter Eleven

Holt handed the police officer at the lab one of his cards. "Here's my contact information."

The officer took the card and nodded. "If we get anything, we'll let you know."

Holt strode down the sidewalk, trying to control his anger. The locks on the back door of the lab were a joke, and security cameras were non-existent. He knew funding for government agencies was minimal at best, but how in the world could they justify such a lack of security at a place testing police evidence?

And the unfortunate tech. He'd be feeling that blow to the head for weeks and be sporting a scar on his forehead the rest of his life, but the poor guy was more upset over the stolen evidence.

Holt was upset over the entire thing.

Alex walked quietly beside him, but she remained wisely silent.

He climbed inside the truck and banged his

hand on the steering wheel. Never had he felt at such a loss. The entire thing was spiraling out of control, and he was further away from answers than he had been the day Erika disappeared.

"I don't understand," Alex said. "Why would someone take the leg?"

"Clearly he didn't want us to identify the body."

Alex sucked in a breath. "They wouldn't have known about the serial number on the pin. They don't know that we already know it's Bobby."

"The only silver lining in this entire mess."

"So what do we do now?"

"We head back to Vodoun. There's nothing left here for us to do."

He started the truck, but as he was about to pull away from the curb, his cell phone rang again. This time, he didn't recognize the telephone number.

"Mr. Chamberlain?" the man said when he answered.

"Yes."

"This is Al Johnson. You came in my pawn shop about that guitar."

"Yes, Mr. Johnson. Have you remembered something else?"

"Even better. I just saw that guy that sold me the guitar walk into a bar on St. Charles Street."

Holt stiffened. "You're sure?"

"Got a clear look at him before he went inside. The Lizard Lounge. Do you want me to do anything?"

"No. If he sees you, he may bolt. Just stay out of sight and call me if you see him leave the bar."

"Got it."

Holt threw his foot down on the accelerator and launched the truck onto the street. As he cut around traffic, he told a startled looking Alex about the phone call.

"Shouldn't you call the police?" she asked.

"If he sees the cops coming, he'll bail."

"But what are you going to do?"

"Confront him, and then call the New Orleans cops. They can book him for me and I'll transport him to Vodoun for holding."

"Confront him? He killed Bobby. I don't think that's a good idea."

"Well, when you figure out how I can arrest him from a distance, let me know. But I have to tell you, that's not going to be nearly as satisfying."

"At least I'll be there to back you up."

Holt shook his head. "Absolutely not. You're

not going anywhere near that bar. You're going to sit in the truck and wait for me to do my job."

"You expect me to sit like some lady-in-waiting?"

"Yes, I do. Despite my allowing you to come along for some of this, you are not a cop and don't have the training necessary to handle something like this. I expect you to respect my ability to do my job."

Alex pursed her lips but didn't argue. He knew he'd get her with the respect comment.

He pulled into an alley behind the bar and parked half a block down from the bar, next to a Dumpster.

"If anyone hassles you, move the truck one street over." He handed her the keys. "Have your cell phone close by. I'll let you know what's happening."

He exited the truck and skirted around the corner of the alley and onto St. Charles Street. The bar was in the center of the street. It was early evening, so it was crowded, but he figured that played in his favor. It was easier to blend in. If the killer knew who he was, he'd immediately know why he was there.

He edged along the wall of the tiny pub, scanning the patrons as he went, but none of them matched the guy from the pawn shop video. Maybe Al Johnson had been mistaken.

He'd seen the guy from across the street. It was possible he'd made the wrong guy.

Suddenly, a crack of light fell across his face and he glanced to the back of the bar in time to see two men at the back entrance. The first man was pushing the door open with his right hand.

The tattoo. It was there on the back of his hand.

The second man was wearing a black hooded sweatshirt with the hood pulled up. He glanced back for a second, but the hood was pulled so far down, Holt couldn't make out any of the man's features.

Suddenly, it hit him that Alex was a sitting duck in the alley.

Holt worked his way through the crowd to the back door, dialing Alex's number as he walked.

"He just walked out the back door of the bar with another man," he said when she answered. "They're in the alley with you. Get out before they see you."

"Too late," Alex said. "I ducked down when the door opened. I don't think they paid attention to the truck since it's partially hidden by the Dumpster, but if I pull away now, they'll bolt."

"Can you see them now?"

"No. There's a stack of crates blocking my

view. I only caught a glimpse of them walking out the back door before I ducked, but I think they're somewhere in those crates."

Holt cursed under his breath. "Stay put and stay low until I call you."

"Be careful."

Holt slipped the phone into his jeans pocket and eased the back door open just a crack. The men weren't anywhere to be seen, but crates and boxes littered the alley. They could be standing mere feet away and still be out of sight.

The faint sound of voices caught his ear and he slipped out into the alley, trying to determine the direction of the voices. An eight-foot stack of crates stood to his right, and he eased up behind them.

The voices grew louder and he peered through the slats in the crates, trying to make out the face of either man. The man from the pawn shop was facing the crates Holt crouched behind and he got a clean look at him. It was definitely the guy he was looking for. The guy with the hooded sweatshirt had his back to the crates, so Holt still couldn't get a look at him.

"I told you to dump the body in the bayou," the man in the hooded sweatshirt said.

"I did," the tattoo man replied.

"Then how did that leg wind up in a police laboratory in New Orleans?"

"Maybe it was the tide. I weighted it down."

"You really messed up, killing that guy."

"It's not my fault the guy saw me grab the kid and followed me. What was I supposed to do—let him go?"

"You were supposed to make sure no one was watching when you grabbed the kid."

"I cleared out his apartment, just like you said, so everyone would think he took off with the kid."

"And that plan would have worked if that fill-in sheriff hadn't found a piece of him lying around. If the cops figure out that Bobby Rhonaldo is dead, they're going to start treating this as something other than a random kidnapping. But all that's irrelevant now, and it's not the only problem I have."

"I did everything you told me to do."

"Yes, and more. I saw the pawn ticket when you paid for lunch. You pawned that guitar, you idiot."

"But no one knows I had the guitar but you," the tattoo man argued, but his expression belied the certainty of his words.

"Rhonaldo is missing, along with his daughter and all his belongings. That guitar was rare. The police could have sent out a bulletin asking anyone who sees it to contact them. Pawn shops don't want any trouble with the law."

"I'm sure no one's looking for it," the man said, his nervousness clear in his voice. "The guy didn't even ask me questions."

"Of course he didn't ask questions. He's not the cops and wouldn't want trouble in his shop, but that doesn't mean he didn't pick up the phone and call the police as soon as you left."

"Maybe the police will think Bobby sold the guitar for cash to get out of town."

"Pawn shops have excellent security systems. If the owner reported the sale to the police, you can bet they have your face plastered across every law enforcement office in Louisiana."

"I…I'm sorry, boss—"

"You would risk this—everything I've worked for—for a couple of dollars? What do you think I ought to do about that? What do you think I will do about that?"

"I'll lie low," tattoo man said, clearly starting to panic. "I have a place out of town. I can go there until this blows over."

"I have a better idea."

"No!" the man screamed.

Holt heard the click of steel but before he could jump around the crates, the shot rang out through the alley.

"Police!" he yelled and vaulted around the

crates, gun leveled, but the shooter was already running down the alley.

Straight toward Alex.

THE SHOOTER DUCKED IN and out of the debris and Dumpsters that lined the alley, making a shot impossible, especially as Holt was dodging the same obstacles. He prayed that Alex had heard the shot and stayed down. He had no doubt that if the shooter saw her, he'd have no problem killing her.

He was about thirty yards from his truck when three more shots rang out.

"No!" He ran as fast as he could, knocking over crates and trash cans as he went.

He rounded the Dumpster and saw steam coming from the engine. Two single bullet holes went straight through the windshield. He scanned the alley for the shooter, but he was long gone.

Holt rushed to the truck and yanked the door open. Alex looked up at him from where she was crouched on the floorboard, her hands and face covered with tiny cuts from the scattering of glass from the windshield. He felt almost dizzy from relief.

"Are you all right?" He extended his hand.

"Yes," she said and took his hand. She stepped out of the truck, then slumped back against it and took a deep breath. "I thought... he came around that corner and before I could even duck, he'd already fired a shot at me. I barely ducked before he shot again."

She started shaking. "If he'd have stopped even a second longer to fire a shot through the door—"

"But he didn't," Holt interrupted. He pulled her into his arms and held her close to him, trying to control his own racing heart. It was just beginning to hit him how close he'd come to losing her.

Alex squeezed him tightly, and he could feel her racing heart beating against his chest. "You were right for telling me to stay behind. I know it didn't turn out like you expected, but it's clear I'm not qualified to handle this."

He placed his hands on each side of her face and looked down at her. "You handled it fine. You're alive. That's the only important thing."

"But he got away. If I'd been better at this, I would have taken out my own gun and shot him in the leg or something."

He smiled. "Old Ms. Maude did not teach you that much in one afternoon."

Alex laughed. "I'm alive."

Holt nodded. "Let's call the police. The other guy wasn't as lucky."

"Oh, no!"

"Did you get a good look at the shooter?"

"No. The hood was low, and it all happened so fast."

"It's okay," he said. "I didn't get a good look, either."

She didn't say any more, but he could tell by her expression that she felt the same way he did—frustrated, disappointed, cheated. Another good lead that had resulted in a dead end. Literally.

But it was hard to remain angry when he thought about what could have been lost. If Alex had reacted a second slower, or the shooter had been just a hair more accurate. He shook his head. Best to remove those thoughts completely from his mind. Alex was safe, and he was going to see that she stayed that way.

It took three long hours to settle everything with the New Orleans Police Department, the coroner and the mechanic's shop. Three long hours to find out that the dead guy carried no identification and his fingerprints weren't in the system. Only thirty minutes to find out that the truck couldn't be repaired that night and they were without transportation.

"So what now?" Alex asked, as they signed off on their written statements.

"It's late, and we're both exhausted. I say we

check into a hotel and get a rental car tomorrow. The repairs on my truck may take a few days."

"Why waste money on a hotel? My apartment is ten minutes from here."

"And that's probably the first place the shooter will look."

The breath caught in her throat for a moment, and she shook her head. "You're right. I guess I'm having trouble wrapping my mind around all the implications." Not to mention trying to control her emotions over the thought of checking into a hotel with Holt. Still, logic overruled emotion every time.

"Separate rooms, of course," she said.

"Of course, but connected. Just in case…"

He didn't finish his sentence, but he didn't have to. She knew Holt was afraid the shooter would come looking for them—her specifically, since he couldn't be certain she hadn't gotten a good look at his face.

"Sir," an officer interrupted them. "The captain asked me to give you a lift wherever you need to go. If you're planning on staying the night, I can recommend a hotel a couple of blocks over."

"That's fine," Holt said. "Thanks."

Twenty minutes later, Holt slid a key card in the hotel door and pushed it open, allowing Alex to step inside. He did a quick sweep of the room, checking the bathroom and closets, then unlocked the door to the adjoining room. He left her room and, just seconds later, stepped back inside through the adjoining door.

"Does it pass inspection?" she asked.

"Yeah. I'm glad they had adjoining rooms on the upper floors. You want to order room service? I'm starving."

"Surprisingly, I am, too, but then I guess with minimal breakfast and almost no lunch, it stands to reason. Even the scared-half-to-death get hungry eventually."

"Hey." Holt placed a hand on her arm. "It's okay to be scared. When I saw him take off in your direction, all I could do was run like hell and pray that you ducked."

"It happened so quickly, yet it seemed like it happened in slow motion. Does that make any sense?"

He frowned. "Yeah. It makes perfect sense."

It looked for a moment like he was going to say more, but then Alex saw the sheet come down over his eyes and knew he'd gone back to that place where everything was protected and nothing got outside of him. It was the brick wall she'd run up against so many times in their relationship. There was no scaling it and no breaking through.

She picked up a room service menu from the

nightstand. "I think I'm going to have a burger and fries. How about you?"

"Sounds good."

She handed him the menu. "Would you mind ordering? I want to take a quick shower."

She slipped into the bathroom and turned on the shower, making sure the water was piping hot. A clean change of clothes would have been great, but the hotel robe would have to do.

The hot water made her sigh as she backed under the showerhead and let it run down her shoulders and back. She felt some of the tension leave her neck as her muscles loosened, and she rotated her head in a circular motion, the vertebrae cracking as she moved.

It was the first time she'd been alone since the shooting. Only the sound of running water surrounded her, and she was able to process everything that had happened that day. It was a lot of processing, but if anyone had the skill to handle it, she did. At least, she hoped she did.

College, medical school, internship—all preparing her to face the most complicated and elevated of emotions. But nothing could prepare you for harnessing all that knowledge and applying it to yourself. Logically, she knew she should be grateful to be alive and she was, but she was scared to death for Erika.

Based on what Holt overheard in the alley,

it seemed fairly certain that the dead man had killed Bobby, pawned the guitar and dumped the body. If he had Erika, God only knew what had happened to her. And Alex was scared for Sarah. Her cousin hadn't even scratched the surface of recovering from her husband's affair and their impending divorce, and now he was dead. If something happened to Erika, Alex didn't know that Sarah would be able to cope.

She ducked her head under the hot stream of water, rinsing the shampoo from her long tresses. If only their problems could be washed away so easily, she thought. She stepped out of the shower and dried off, twisting her damp hair into a knot at the back of her head, then donned a hotel robe and took a final look at herself in the foggy mirror.

Considering what she'd been through that day, she didn't look bad. A little pale, but then, that could also be from not eating. At least, that was what she would tell herself. She applied a bit of the moisturizer sample provided by the hotel to her face and pronounced herself fit for eating inside her hotel room.

The food had already arrived and was waiting on a small table in her room next to the window. Holt was nowhere in sight. She peeked through the door to his room and saw the bathroom door closed. Before she could back away from the doorway, the bathroom door flew open and Holt stepped out, drying his hair with a towel.

He'd put on his same jeans, but he was bare everywhere else. Alex couldn't help but notice how much harder his body was, and she longed to run her hand across his exposed skin. She also saw the scars. Some were scratches, and at least one looked like it was a puncture wound or perhaps a bullet hole. She sucked in a breath. The boy who'd left had come back a man. A man who'd probably seen more tragedy than she could ever imagine.

He lowered the towel and saw her standing there. "You okay?"

"Yeah," she said, yanking her gaze from his body up to his face. She could feel a flush creeping up her chest and neck.

He grinned and she knew he'd known that she was studying his body. A body she used to know every square inch of, but now was so different. For just a second, she wondered if his body would still fit with hers the way it used to—as if they'd been cast from molds intended to be separate pieces of the same item. But she dashed that thought away as soon as it appeared. Emotions were running high right now. Making decisions in such highly charged emotional states usually led to disaster.

"I put the food on the table in your room," he said. "It's bigger than the one in mine."

"I saw and I smelled, and I can't wait to dive in."

Holt nodded. "No matter the stress level, eventually the body requires fuel." He stepped forward until he was standing directly in front of her. She could feel the heat coming off of his body, and she longed to place a single hand on his bare chest, just like she used to.

Startled at her own lack of self-control, she stepped back and crossed the room to take a seat at the table. "Guess we better get to this before it gets cold."

Chapter Twelve

Holt didn't move from the doorway for a couple of seconds, and Alex could feel his eyes on her. But instead of looking at him, she focused on arranging the plates and adding salt to her food.

"It looks good," she said.

Holt laughed and crossed the room to take a seat across from her. "You really are hungry when hotel food looks good."

Alex smiled, feeling a bit more relaxed now that there was a table in between them. "I suppose you're right." She popped a fry in her mouth and was surprised how good it tasted. "It's hard to mess up a burger, though."

"Some still manage."

Alex nodded. "So?" she said, now that the small talk about food was out of the way.

Holt finished his bite of burger, then took a big drink of soda. "'So' is the question."

"I don't understand how the man who killed Bobby wasn't in the system. I doubt he's a rogue banker or accountant. If he was a career criminal, why no record of him?"

"Maybe he's very careful."

"But he pawned the guitar? That doesn't sound very careful."

"No, but based on the conversation I overheard, the guy that got away was pulling the strings. Maybe up until now, the dead guy followed orders to a tee. Maybe he got too confident and decided he knew better than those giving the orders."

"But that would mean he's part of something bigger. Something organized if he's been at this all his adult life, unless you think he and the guy that got away are the only two working together."

"Could be."

"But you don't think so."

"No. It doesn't feel right, somehow."

"And all of this is tied to someone in Vodoun." Alex blew out a breath. "It doesn't seem possible."

"I know."

"That tattoo on his hand. Does it mean anything?"

She studied Holt's face. She knew there was something about that tattoo that he wasn't telling her, and she wanted to know what it was.

He focused on his food, not answering.

"You know something," she pushed. "I could tell by your expression and body language when we left the pawn shop that something was eating at you. You must have seen that tattoo on the pawn shop video and realized it meant something then. Why are you keeping something from me?"

Holt sighed. "Because everything's not about you."

"If that man took Erika and you know something about the tattoo that could help us find her, then it *is* my concern."

He stared directly at her, his indecision clear, and Alex felt her pulse spike just a bit. What in the world was he hiding that had him so worried?

"I've seen the tattoo before. Long before Erika was even born."

"Where?"

"On the man who murdered my father."

The bottled water slipped from her hand and crashed to the floor. A cold chill ran over her body, and she covered her mouth with both hands.

"No!" she said. "Oh, Holt." She reached across the table to place her hand on his. "How did you... I didn't know you saw..."

"No one knows."

She stared. "What about the police? Surely you told them—"

"The police didn't want to hear the ravings of a ten-year-old boy who was scared half to death and claimed to see a strange man leaving their garage in the middle of the day, especially as I was skipping school with Max and Tanner and they figured we were making the whole thing up to get out of trouble."

"Max and Tanner saw it, too?"

"No. We were racing our bikes and I got there first. By the time they pulled up behind me in the bushes, the man was already gone.

"We thought we were being so sneaky," he continued, "climbing up the tree out back and into my bedroom window that I'd left unlocked that morning. I already had a stash of comics, chips and Coke and we spent the whole afternoon there, mostly to avoid a math test."

He stared at the wall behind her and blew out a breath. "And all that time, our dad was in the living room below us, bleeding out onto Mom's 'good' rug. We had no idea. Even today, it still doesn't seem right somehow."

"You never went downstairs," Alex rationalized, "and besides, your dad wasn't even living there any longer. You had no reason to think he'd be in the house, much less—"

"I think it was one of those times he and

Mom were 'talking' about their relationship again. Anytime he had a fight with Tanner's mother, he came crawling back to mine."

Holt sighed. "He was our father. Granted, he was also a cheater, a workaholic and rarely even acknowledged that he had children, but he was still our father. He was slipping quietly from this world, not ten feet below us, and yet we didn't sense anything."

For the first time in her life, and despite having years of training to deal with intense emotional situations, Alex had no words. The horror and frustration he must have felt as a young boy, knowing that he had vital information about his dad's murder, but with no adult to give it credence. Instead, he'd carried it around, tucked deep inside of him all these years. And she'd never known. She was beginning to wonder how well she'd ever known Holt.

"I'm so sorry," she said finally. "I don't suppose you tried telling anyone when you got older?"

"No. The old sheriff didn't retire until a few years ago, and even if I'd have insisted on what I saw, he still would have thought it was the frightened, confused memories of a boy who had lost his father."

"But now your uncle is in charge." Alex stared at him, as a thought flashed across her mind. "You're not filling in for your uncle to help him out, are you? You wanted access to your dad's case files."

"A lot of good it did. There wasn't any more to see than what I already knew."

"The sheriff didn't investigate the murder?"

"Oh, he investigated. He wasted a whole lot of time compiling paper after paper of useless information on mine, Max and Tanner's mothers. Like any of them would have done this. Despite the way he treated them, they all loved him and none of them would have hurt their children that way."

She nodded. Despite the many shortcomings of all three women and their strange attraction to a man who wouldn't commit to any of them for any length of time, none would have done anything to hurt their children—not intentionally, anyway. They simply never stopped to consider that allowing Walt Conroy to bounce back and forth into their lives *did* hurt the children.

"I changed my last name to my mother's maiden name because I didn't want to be anything like him. He hurt so many people with his selfishness, and his murder was the final blow. Whatever he was mixed up in cost everyone who loved him, but I bet he didn't think twice about his family before getting involved. That's just the way he was."

Holt stared out the hotel window for a bit, and Alex could tell a million thoughts were running through his head. Finally, he turned his gaze back to her. "That's why I left Vodoun."

Alex stared. "I don't understand."

"I left because I didn't want to hurt you, the way my dad hurt mine and my brothers' mothers. The way my grandfather hurt Lorraine. I watched my mother grieve every time he changed his mind again, and it killed me. I felt every tear she shed."

He looked directly at her. "I figured it was better to leave then before you cared so much you wasted your entire life over it."

"What your dad and grandfather did was a choice. No one forced them to play with their families that way."

"I know, but I wasn't ready to settle down and didn't know that I ever would be. But you were so certain...so sure you wanted me. I wasn't sure, and I didn't want you to hurt the way my mom did."

"So you left," Alex said, her mind spinning with Holt's admission. "And broke my heart in two."

"It was the only thing I knew to do at the time. I needed space from you, from my mom and from the memories of my father. I needed to figure out what I wanted for the rest of my life, and creating responsibilities was the last thing I wanted at the time."

As much as it pained her to hear him speak those words, she knew she had to ask him the one question burning inside of her, even if she didn't like the answer. "So did it work? Did you get me out of your system so that you could move on?"

He rose from his chair. "No. And I don't think I ever will."

He leaned over and lowered his lips to hers.

She knew it was a mistake. One she would end up regretting, but at that moment she couldn't think of one single reason to push him away, or resist when he pulled her up from the chair and pressed every inch of his body against hers.

He caressed her lips with his, then gently pushed inside her mouth with his tongue. Her skin tingled as he slipped the robe off her shoulders and it slid to the floor. She gasped when he trailed kisses down her neck, across her chest and finally took a swollen nipple into his mouth. She thought about asking him to slow down, make it last longer, but already her body was begging for the release only Holt had ever been able to give her.

Her skin warmed as he started a fire in her center that spread through every inch of her body, and she longed to have her hands on him again. She unfastened his jeans and pushed them over his narrow hips. Trailing her hands down his chest, she marveled at how familiar, yet different, his body felt. It was a thickened, firmer body of a man rather than the boy who'd left.

He moaned when she took the length of him into her palm, and whispered, "Protection?"

Alex stepped away long enough to retrieve her purse from the nightstand and pull out a condom. "I'm a doctor. I'm always prepared," she said.

Holt lifted her up in his arms and placed her gently on the bed. "Thank God for that," he said and lowered himself on top of her, kissing her deeply, with a hunger she'd longed for over a decade.

Her hips moved upward, inviting his body into hers, yearning for the union that she'd missed for so long. When he entered her, she felt her body contract around him and the first wave of pleasure washed over her. Slowly he moved deeper inside of her and she clutched his back, unable to hold back the fire building inside her again.

Minutes later, he sent them both over the edge.

His body was heavy on hers as it pulsed with pleasure. At that moment, it felt as if they'd never been apart, and she couldn't help but wish that the moment would never end.

HOLT AWAKENED BEFORE SUNRISE, Alex nestled against him, still in a deep slumber. He knew last night had been a mistake, but also knew that given an opportunity to redo the entire thing, he still would have made the same decision.

Even though it wasn't fair to Alex.

He'd known from the first moment he'd seen her again that his feelings were real. That time had only made them stronger, not diminished them as he'd figured would happen. But his return into her life was at the worst possible time. Even a woman as strong as Alex couldn't make a good decision under this much stress.

The appropriate thing to do was to back off and give her some room. When the crisis was over, and if she still felt the same, then they could talk. But for now, he needed to focus on one single objective—finding Erika.

He eased out of bed and pulled on his jeans, then grabbed his T-shirt and tennis shoes from the other room—the room they hadn't really needed. He cast one last glance at her before slipping out of the room and into the hallway.

The mechanic at the garage had assured Holt he'd be in the shop when the rental car company next door opened at six a.m. He needed to speak to the mechanic about the repairs to his truck and rent a car to get them back to Vodoun. With any luck, he'd be back before Alex noticed he was gone.

ALEX ROLLED OVER IN BED and reached out with her arm, but all she found in her reach was cold sheets. She opened her eyes and glanced around the room, but there was no sign of Holt. A quick look at the alarm clock on the nightstand told her it was barely seven a.m.

She rose from the bed and pulled on the hotel robe. There was no sign of Holt in the other room but his clothes were gone.

She plopped back down on the edge of the bed, trying to control her disappointment. Even though she knew there was probably a completely necessary and logical explanation for his absence, she couldn't help but feel as if the distance was back between them—physically and emotionally.

Last night had been incredible. All her memories of how it felt to be in Holt's arms didn't even do justice to the real thing. After all these years without him, he drew her right back in, body and soul.

Surely, he'd felt it, too.

She lifted the phone from the nightstand and ordered coffee and some croissants from room service, then pulled on her clothes from the day before, wishing she had a clean set. She'd just finished tying her tennis shoes when she heard the door latch click and Holt walked in.

"I thought you'd still be asleep," he said.

"I'm not much of a late sleeper, especially in a strange bed."

Holt nodded. "The mechanic says it will take a few days to fix my truck. I rented us a car to get back to Vodoun."

Alex watched him closely as he gave her the information. He stood just inside the door, not making a move to close the distance between them. His delivery contained no more emotion than it would if he were delivering just the facts to anyone.

He regrets it.

The thought ripped through her mind unbidden and she felt a blush begin at her chest and creep up her neck. How could she be so stupid? Thinking Holt Chamberlain had changed? Thinking he cared about anyone else but himself?

At least, given the situation with Sarah and Erika, she had an excuse for her lapse in judgment. Holt didn't have a single one. He'd known exactly what he was doing last night. Known exactly how she would respond.

Damn him.

Well, if he thought that she was going to waste her time trying to convince him to care about her, he had another think coming. Two could play the calm-and-cool game.

"I ordered breakfast. Just coffee and croissants. I figured you'd want to get on the road as soon as possible."

"Yeah. You know, with everything that's happened, we're going to have to tell Sarah about Bobby. If not, she's going to hear it from someone else. Too many people are talking now."

"I know. I'll give my friend a call on the way to Vodoun and see how Sarah's doing. That way I can formulate a plan for telling her. I assume you don't have a problem with my delivering that information?"

He looked a bit surprised but shook his head. "No, not at all. I can be there, though—"

"That's not necessary. I can handle it."

"Whatever you think," he said, but she could tell that he was a bit put off and confused over her dismissal.

He started to say something else, when a knock sounded at the door. He opened the door and an attendant pushed a room service cart into the room. When he'd gone, Alex poured a cup of coffee into a cardboard cup and pulled a croissant from the stack.

"I figure we can eat on the road, right? No sense delaying what I have to do today."

She slung her purse over her shoulder and walked past Holt to exit the room. She could feel his eyes on her, but he didn't make a move to stop her and never said a word.

And that said it all.

THIRTY MINUTES LATER, they were halfway to Vodoun and neither had spoken another word. Alex downed the last of her coffee and slipped the empty cup into the cup holder on the center console. She'd taken her time consuming the croissant and coffee to ensure she had something to occupy her body and mind, but now that her hands were empty, the silence in the car was deafening.

You are being just as childish as him.

She looked out the windshield and down the long, flat, empty highway and sighed. Sometimes being so logical and fair was a real pain. Glancing over at Holt, she tried to guess what he was thinking, but couldn't narrow in on a single thing. She expected to see his famous scowl, but was surprised when his expression was more contemplative.

Then she realized he was glancing in the mirrors every couple of seconds.

"We're being followed," he said.

"Are you sure? Never mind. Of course you're sure. How long?"

Holt pressed the accelerator down and the car leaped forward. "Probably since New Orleans, but I didn't pick up the tail in all the traffic leaving the city."

"It's him, right? Who else would it be?" Alex scanned the deserted highway for any sign of life, but they were miles away from the nearest town. Dark clouds swirled overhead, seeming to mirror the ominous situation on the ground.

She pulled her cell phone from her purse and cursed when she saw no signal. She turned around in her seat to look back and gasped when she saw that the black sedan rapidly gaining on them.

"Can you go faster?"

"Not in this rental."

"How far to the next town?"

"Ten miles. Hold on," Holt said. "He's going to hit us."

A second later, the sedan slammed into their rental car from behind. Alex jolted forward, and the seat belt cut across her chest, digging into her skin. Holt clenched the steering wheel, struggling to maintain control of the car.

Alex glanced into the side mirror and saw the sedan about ten feet behind and approaching rapidly on the passenger's side.

Holt swerved, attempting to cut off the sedan before it could draw alongside them, but the rental car's engine was no match for the sedan. Alex watched in horror as the sedan drew alongside them and slammed into the side of their rental.

Holt struggled to keep the car straight on the highway, but didn't stand a chance against the force of the hit. The car slid sideways toward the center median. Holt turned the wheel to correct the slide, but as the back end of the car slid around, the sedan clipped it again, just on the edge, sending the car into a spin.

Alex lost all sense of direction as the car spun, but a flash of water sent her into a panic. They were headed straight for the drainage ditch that ran parallel to the highway. The very large, very deep, very full drainage ditch.

She couldn't stop herself from screaming as the car plunged over the edge.

Chapter Thirteen

As soon as the car hit the water, Alex released her seat belt and opened her eyes, trying to make out anything in the darkness. She was relieved to see Holt alert beside her but began to panic when she pushed on the door and it wouldn't open.

"I'm going to kick the window out," Holt said as water began to pour into the car from all available cracks. "Get ready to hold your breath and swim."

Alex nodded, trying not to think about what was waiting for them at the surface. Holt leaned sideways in the driver's seat and gave the driver's-side window one hard kick.

Water poured into the car and Alex held her breath as it rushed over her head. She opened her eyes in the murky blackness, but could only see inches in front of her. Reaching out with her hand, she felt Holt's shoes as he swam out of the window. A couple of seconds later, she felt the opening and pushed herself through, kicking her way up to the surface.

As soon as she broke the surface, she gasped for air and looked for Holt. The dirty water blurred her vision, but she could see him within arm's distance, scanning the bank above them. She looked up at the bank, already afraid of what she'd see, and choked back a scream as she looked straight into the black eyes of a crow on the embankment above her.

The crow stared for a second, then vaulted from the bank to fly into the swamp behind them. She scanned the bank for any sign of the killer and was shocked to find it completely empty.

Holt had surfaced a couple of feet from where she did and she looked over at him. "Where did he go?"

"I don't know, but we need to get out of here while we have the chance." He pointed to a section of the bank about twenty feet away that was sloped enough for them to climb out of the ditch.

Alex swam to the sloped embankment and began to pull herself up. Clutching the tufts of marsh grass, she pushed with her feet, sliding in the slick Louisiana mud. Her biceps burned as she inched her way up the bank until she could peer over the lip of the embankment. She scanned the highway for any sign of their attacker, but there was no sign of the black sedan as far as she could see. She made one last effort to pull herself over the lip and onto the shoulder of the highway, then looked over just in time to see Holt scrambling over the edge next to her.

"He's gone," she said. "Why would he leave when he had us trapped?"

Holt pointed behind her. "That's why."

Alex turned to look and almost collapsed with relief when she saw a police car barreling toward them.

"Someone must have passed on the opposite side of the highway and saw him hit us. He probably figured they'd call the police as soon as they could, and he couldn't risk getting caught. There's not many turnoffs on this highway."

Holt rose from the ground and extended his hand to Alex to help her up. "Are you all right?" he asked, scanning her for injuries.

"A little shaken, but okay," she said. "Did you see the crow?" A chill passed over her as she looked into the swamp where the crow had disappeared.

Before he could respond, the squad car screeched to a stop next to them.

An officer jumped out and rushed over to them. "Do I need to call for an ambulance?"

"No," Holt assured him. "We're fine, given the circumstances."

"A trucker called in and said he saw you being run off the road." The officer glanced into the ditch. "Is your car in there?"

"Yes," Holt said, "and the rental company is not going to be pleased."

"Do you think the other driver was drunk?"

"No. This was intentional."

The officer's eyes widened. "The trucker gave me a description of the car, but didn't know the model. Did you get a good enough look to determine that?"

"It was a late-model Cadillac."

"What about the driver? Can you give me a description at all?"

Alex shook her head. "The windows were tinted so dark, you couldn't see inside."

The officer blew out a breath. "I've already called ahead and have two state troopers looking for the sedan, but the nearest trooper was forty miles up the highway from here. If he's smart, he could take any one of several opportunities to turn off the highway before then."

"My guess is he's a professional," Holt said. "I don't think your troopers will catch sight of him."

The officer stared at Holt. "Sounds like I have a story to hear, but first, I need to get

you two off of the highway and into some dry
clothes. My office is back about fifteen miles,
and there's a Wal-Mart across the street. We
can get you something to wear while I get all
this on paper. If that's all right with you, of
course."

Holt looked over at Alex and she nodded.
"That's fine, but I'd really appreciate it if we
could make it as quick as possible. We were
on our way to Vodoun to tell my cousin that
her estranged husband was murdered—likely
by the same man who just ran us off the road
and has kidnapped her six-year-old daughter."

"Is your cousin alone?"

"No. A friend of mine who is a nurse is staying with her, but I don't want her to hear about
this from someone else. And given the situation, I'm worried about their safety."

"Rightfully so," the officer said. "I'll call
from the car and get someone sent to watch
your cousin's house. I'll send an unmarked vehicle, so hopefully it won't alarm your cousin."

"I really appreciate that," Alex said, feeling
a bit of relief that Sarah would have police protection.

The officer motioned to his car and she and
Holt slid into the backseat. Lightning flashed
overhead and she jumped, all of her nerves still

on edge. Holt reached across the seat and took her hand in his.

"We're going to get through this," he said. "I promise you."

Alex nodded and looked straight ahead. She appreciated his support in all this more than anything, but suspected that once the crisis was over, Holt would move on to the next phase of his life.

Just like he had before.

"No!" THE BLOOD RUSHED from Sarah's face and she covered her mouth with both hands, staring at Alex with wide eyes. It took only a moment for the tears to brim up and well over. Then her cousin collapsed into a heap in her arms.

"Why Bobby?" Sarah wailed. "He never hurt anyone but me."

Alex held Sarah close to her. "I know. I'm so sorry."

"Why is this happening? Where is my baby?"

Alex looked over at Holt, who stood just inside the living room doorway. His expression was a mixture of sadness and anger, and she couldn't help but wonder if he was thinking about all the times his own mother had cried over his father, or maybe the soldiers he'd known who had died, and the families they'd left behind.

"We're going to find Erika," Alex reassured her. "I made a promise to you and I intend to keep it."

Sarah looked up at her. "But what if he hurts you, too? You're all I have left, Alex. My entire family is disappearing and I can't do anything to stop it."

Alex gave her a squeeze. "I'm not going anywhere."

But even as she said the words, she had a flicker of doubt. Whatever was going on was so much bigger than what she'd originally imagined. It was organized, and the people behind it were ruthless, and now it was clear they had Alex and Holt in their sights.

Everything they did from this point forward would have to be even more carefully calculated and measured than before. But Alex wasn't about to give up. The killer probably thought he'd scared them away, but he'd only strengthened their resolve.

"I want you to stop," Sarah said. "I can't ask Holt to because he's the acting sheriff, but you're not law enforcement and don't need to put yourself at risk any longer."

"I'm fine," Alex reassured her, infinitely glad she and Holt had decided not to tell Sarah about being run off the road. "If I can do something to help, I'm going to continue. I promise I'll be extra careful. We both will be."

Sarah's bottom lip quivered as she looked over at Holt, who nodded. As Sarah looked back at her, tears streaming down her cheeks, Alex knew her cousin's mind and heart was warring between wanting Alex involved because she believed in her ability to fix anything and wanting to lock the front door and keep her safe.

Finally, Sarah looked back at Holt and said, "If you let anything happen to her, Holt Chamberlain, I'll haunt you forever."

Holt's jaw set in a hard line. "I will do anything necessary to keep her safe."

HOLT PULLED THE CAR in front of the grocery store and looked over at Alex. "I'm just going to make some notes at the station and call my uncle. I'm sure he's heard what's going on through the grapevine, and I need to do some damage control. Call me when you're ready to be picked up, but don't leave the store."

He figured she'd argue, as Alex was the last woman in the world to be told what to do, but she simply nodded and climbed out of the car. Holt watched as she made her way inside the store and let loose the string of curses he'd been holding in for hours. The situation was taking a toll on all of them. He'd never seen Alex so defeated, and it bothered him more than he'd ever thought possible.

He understood her despair. As a doctor, all her education, training and time was spent fixing things, but this was a situation she couldn't fix. He'd had to deal with the same issues in the military. As a leader, he had a mission to accomplish and a goal to keep his men safe. Every failure felt like a metal stake through the heart.

Sighing, he put the car in gear and pulled away from the curb. His uncle had already left six messages on his cell phone—each increasing in volume—and he wasn't looking forward to the ensuing conversation. Given that he'd cajoled his uncle into going along with the investigation to begin with, Holt knew he had a lot to answer for.

If he could just find the answers in the next five minutes, that would be great.

His phone rang again and he glanced at the display. His uncle. Knowing he couldn't put the ensuing conversation off any longer, he answered the call.

"Uncle Conroy," Holt said. "What a surprise."

"Don't give me that. I've got calls from the insurance company telling me the department gets to pay for damage to your truck and a

totaled rental car. You're running my department and good name into the ground in this
town, not to mention costing the taxpayers God
knows how much money with this so-called
investigation of yours. I want you off this case
and I mean now."

"I can't do that."

"You can and you will. Simply make a note
in the file that Bobby Rhonaldo took off with
his daughter and let the federal agencies handle it."

"Bobby Rhonaldo is dead."

There was complete silence for a couple of
seconds and then Holt heard his uncle cursing.

"Tell me it was anything but murder," his
uncle said finally.

"I'm sorry, but I can't do that." Holt filled his
uncle in on the events that had transpired over
the past couple of days. Aside from the occa-
sional expletive, his uncle didn't interrupt his
monologue.

When he finally finished, he heard his uncle
sigh. "What the hell is going on? This is a
nice town with mostly nice people. Kidnappings, murder, organized crime…that's not the
Vodoun I know."

"It's not the town I know, either, but something's not right here." Holt took a breath and
pushed forward with his next statement before

he could change his mind. "I'm beginning to think the police were looking in the wrong direction back when those girls disappeared. What if all this is somehow connected?"

"That was thirty-six years ago. You honestly believe that something this evil, of this magnitude, has existed here all this time, and no one ever noticed? That *I* never noticed?"

"Maybe it's all organized by someone above reproach."

"Like who?"

"The minister, the bank manager, the guy who owns the grocery store."

"You're kidding, right?"

"No. Think about it. For someone to pull off something this organized for this long, it has to be the last person you would suspect."

"I'm sorry, Holt. I just can't believe that Vodoun has been housing someone that disturbed and no one's ever noticed. I appreciate all the thought you've put into this, especially as it's turned out to be a real mare's nest, but I just can't get on board with your ideas."

"Do you have any better ones?"

"It must be an outsider."

"A stranger who knew about the kidnappings thirty-six years ago and re-created that hype? A stranger who knew Bobby was Erika's father even though he was separated from Sarah and didn't even live in the same home? And why kill him? Why kidnap Erika?"

Holt blew out a breath of frustration. "I can appreciate how much you don't want to wrap your mind around this, but I can't see it as anything but personal. Something is going on here besides your basic child abduction. And I'm going to get to the bottom of it—with or without the backing of the department."

"If you want to investigate your friends and family, go right ahead, but I'm washing my hands of this. When this turns out badly, I will not take any responsibility for the fallout."

"I never assumed anything else."

Holt ended the call and pulled into the sheriff's department parking lot. His uncle was capable enough for speeders and illegal hunters, but when it came to anything remotely serious, he was as useless as Holt had figured he'd be.

Truth be known, it had been a shock to him when he'd gotten the letter from his mother telling him about his uncle's election to sheriff. He'd always considered his uncle to be rather fearful and lazy. Law enforcement didn't exactly suit his disposition, but then, if you didn't actually do anything, perhaps it did. He guessed that more than anything, Jasper liked to use the title to lord over the residents of Vodoun. Growing up in Lorraine's shadow had left Jasper always looking for a way to get the upper hand. Apparently, he'd found it.

Holt entered the office and unlocked the desk, removing a folder that his uncle didn't know the contents of. The folder on his dad. Jasper couldn't even admit that the situation with Bobby and Erika was local and personal. No way would he jump on board with a ring of highly organized killers that had also been responsible for his dad's murder.

But Holt knew all of it was connected. He could feel it in his bones.

Somewhere, in all these seemingly mismatched pieces, was a picture that would eventually take shape. And he was going to keep pushing until it did. His dad had gone too long without justice. His sons had gone too long without answers.

They were all due some peace.

ALEX PUSHED HER CART down the bread aisle, glad she'd made a grocery list at Sarah's house. Her mind was so overloaded, she would have stood there for hours without having a clue what they needed otherwise. Like the last time, when she'd returned to Sarah's with enough tomatoes to feed a small nation.

She selected a loaf of bread and some rolls, then checked her list. Milk was the only item remaining and then she'd be ready to check out. She'd call Holt when she got in line, figuring that would put him at the store by the time she got through paying.

As she rounded the corner to the dairy section, she saw Lorraine Conroy standing at the bakery counter. Given an opportunity, Alex would have turned and left without the milk, just to avoid the woman. Her emotions were too raw and she was too on edge to deal with the shallow accusations of the biggest bitch in Vodoun. But before she could even make a move to wheel the cart around, Lorraine turned around and locked her gaze on Alex.

"Well," Lorraine said, "grocery shopping for your cousin again? Best be careful—men don't like fat women. Or maybe the two of you plan on living out your lives together."

"Commenting on fat women seems a strange statement coming from the woman standing at the bakery counter."

Lorraine laughed. "This is not for me. It's Martin's birthday."

"And you're getting him a cake. How cute. Just like you would for any little boy."

Lorraine's face turned beet-red. "At least I can keep a man."

"It's a shame you didn't know how when your husband was around." Alex knew what she said was a cheap shot before the words even left her mouth, but three decades of insults from Lorraine overrode any manners she had left.

She knew the slap was coming as soon as the words left her mouth, but before Lorraine's hand could connect with her face, Alex caught her wrist. Lorraine yanked her hand from Alex's grasp.

"Why don't you and your cousin leave? Vodoun would be a better place without your kind around."

Lorraine whirled around and hurried away from the bakery counter, the cake long forgotten. A clap of thunder boomed overhead and the lights flickered. Alex grabbed a carton of milk and shoved it in her cart. If she hurried, they might make it back to Sarah's before the storm hit full force.

She hurried to the front of the store, but drew up short as she caught sight of a man running across the street away from the store. It was him. The height, the build, the gait. It was the killer.

Chapter Fourteen

Alex fumbled in her purse for her phone and pressed in Holt's number. "He's here," she said. "Right outside the grocery store."

"Who's there?" Holt asked.

"The killer. I just saw him run across the street."

"Stay inside," Holt said. "I'm pulling up to the store now."

Alex placed her groceries on the conveyor belt and tried to appear normal as the clerk rang her up. She handed the clerk cash and impatiently waited as the clerk counted out the change. Holt was still nowhere in sight when she grabbed her bags and hurried out of the store, completely ignoring Holt's order to stay inside.

She looked up and down the street but didn't see Holt's rental car or the killer. Rain began to fall, and she held one hand over her forehead to keep the huge drops from falling into her eyes.

She was just about to step back into the store when she caught sight of Holt hurrying up the sidewalk a block away.

She rushed down the sidewalk to meet him. "Why didn't you park in front of the store?"

"I saw a man running down the alley a block away. I followed him thinking it might be the man you saw." He pointed a block away to an alley and took one of the grocery stacks from her. "I'm parked there. What was he wearing?"

The rain began to come down heavier and she hurried beside him down the street toward the alley he'd indicated. "Black slacks and a rain jacket. I only saw him from behind, but he moved just like the guy in the alley." She blew out a breath of frustration. "I know that sounds stupid—"

"No, it doesn't."

"What was the guy in the alley wearing?"

"Black slacks and a rain jacket."

Alex felt her pulse spike. "Did you see his face?"

"Yeah." He frowned.

"Do you know who it was?"

"Martin Rommel."

She sucked in a breath and climbed into the car. "Lorraine's boyfriend? You're sure?"

"I've only seen him once, but it was him. I'm sure. He drove away in her Mercedes."

A million thoughts ran through her mind. "But what…why? Sarah only knows the man by sight and reputation, and he and Bobby would hardly move in the same circles. Besides, Rommel's not old enough to have kidnapped those girls years ago."

"No, but I believe this is some type of organized crime. Rommel could easily be the next generation of hired guns."

"But hired to accomplish what, exactly? What in the world is going on here?"

"I don't know, but if Rommel is the killer, I have to wonder what he's up to with Lorraine."

"She's a good cover for him," Alex said. "Wealthy and carries some weight in Vodoun."

"Above reproach," he said. "I tried to tell my uncle earlier that someone local was involved. Someone above reproach, but he didn't want to hear it."

"Well, he's really not going to want to hear this."

"He's not going to."

"But don't you think—"

"I think if I tell my uncle that Rommel's involved, he won't believe a word of it, then he'll tell his mother."

"Who'll tell Rommel," she finished, and sighed. "You know how I feel about Lorraine, but she needs to be warned."

"Not until we're sure." Holt stared silently out the windshield into the pouring rain for several seconds. "Do you know what Rommel does for Lorraine, exactly? I know there's gossip, but my uncle claims their relationship is business. I don't buy it, but what business does he take care of?"

"I don't know. I doubt Sarah does, either, but I wouldn't want to ask her even if I thought she did. She's hanging on by a thread, and if I give her a tangent to launch onto, I'm not sure she'd make sound decisions."

"You think she'd go after him?"

"If she believed for a minute that he was responsible for Bobby's death and Erika's kidnapping, I think she would in a heartbeat."

Holt blew out a breath. "Yeah. I guess I wouldn't blame her. So is there anyone we can ask who won't gossip about it?"

"Ms. Maude."

"Is she going to shoot me if I step onto her land? Her reputation for disliking men is sorta legendary in these parts."

"Ms. Maude doesn't like people as a species. Added to that, she has a low tolerance for stupid and there's plenty of that around."

"She's sort of a hermit. Do you really think she'll know anything that can help?"

"I don't think she misses much. Be honest

with her about what we're doing, and I think she'll tell you anything she knows."

Holt started the car. "Ms. Maude's it is, then."

THE GRAVEL ROAD THAT LED to Ms. Maude's house was narrow, rutted and barely passable with a vehicle. Holt tried not to cringe at the sound of tree branches scraping down the side of his second rental car of the week. His brief foray into law enforcement had been hell on vehicles. The moss-heavy trees draped over the road like a canopy and combined with the storm, made visibility almost nil. It seemed like forever before he finally saw a light from her house ahead.

They jumped from the car and ran to the porch but were still drenched by the time they got there. Before Holt could even lift a hand to knock, the door swung open and he found himself staring down the wrong end of a shotgun.

He stepped back, certain Alex had made a grave miscalculation in suggesting they question Ms. Maude. The woman was a tiny thing, but when you were holding the right end of a shotgun, size became far less important. Her silver hair was cut short and stuck out in all directions and she studied him with a cold, calculating stare.

"What do you want?" she asked.

"Ms. Maude," Alex said, "it's Alexandria Bastin. You taught me to shoot a nine-millimeter this week, remember? I'm Christine Bastin's daughter."

Ms. Maude looked in Alex's direction and squinted. A couple seconds later, her expression switched to one of recognition. "What the hell are you doing standing out here in the storm? Best come inside before you drown."

She lowered the shotgun and motioned them in the house. Holt stepped inside, praying that Alex hadn't missed the mark in labeling Ms. Maude safe and relatively sane.

Ms. Maude's house was a study in contrast from its owner. Dainty lace doilies perched on top of antique tables, with crystal bowls and vases on top of them. Everything was neat with military precision, and Holt felt his spirits rise a bit as they followed her into the kitchen. Perhaps Alex was right. A person this organized physically may also possess a very organized mind.

"I was just making a pot of coffee," Ms. Maude said. "Would you like a cup?"

"I would love a cup," Alex said. She waved a hand at him. "This is Holt Chamberlain. He's filling in for the sheriff while he's out with a broken leg."

Ms. Maude slid two cups of coffee in front

of them and narrowed her eyes at Holt. "You Walt Conroy's boy?"

"Yes, ma'am."

"From which woman—first, second or however many was after?"

"The first."

Ms. Maude nodded. "Your dad was a smart businessman but stupid about relationships. Drove those women crazy and probably would have continued to their entire lives because they would have allowed it."

"You're probably right."

"Wasn't right to do you boys that way, though. Grown women's got a choice. Kids don't."

"I agree with you, ma'am."

"Well, seems you turned out to be a decent sort despite not having a good role model, so what brings you here in the middle of a storm to talk to an old woman? I ain't broke any laws— not that your fool of an uncle would know if I did it in front of him. But I figure you got something on your mind if you came all the way out here in the storm."

"We need your help," Alex said.

"Is this about your missing niece?"

"Yes."

Ms. Maude nodded. "I'll help any way I can. When I think of how scared that poor child must be…well, it just makes me want to haul out my shotgun and put it to good use. What is it you need to know?"

"I want to know everything you can tell me about Martin Rommel," Holt said.

Ms. Maude raised her eyebrows. "Well, I guess I know now why you're here. Can't have everyone knowing you're checking up on Lorraine's bit of fluff, can you?"

"No, ma'am."

"You're shrewd to guess that anyone besides me would probably take that bit of information back to her, but I got no problem telling it how it is and keeping my mouth shut about it besides."

"I'd appreciate anything you can tell me."

"The man's a snake," Ms. Maude said, "and a liar."

"How do you know?"

"I got a feeling for such things, and I didn't like him the moment I set eyes on him. Never had feelings so strong for someone before except a man I met in a bar in New Orleans when I was young and foolish. That man turned out to be a serial killer who was looking to make me his victim that night. If I hadn't listened to my instincts, I wouldn't be talking to you today. That taught me to never ignore what I feel."

Holt nodded. "You're smart to do so. My

uncle said Rommel's relationship with Lorraine is about business, but do you know what that business is?"

Ms. Maude snorted. "Business, my foot. The woman's got him hanging around like a plaything. Oh, she cooked up some story about him running her high-end restaurant...years of experience and a culinary degree and the like. I ate there a couple of times and one thing is for certain—Martin Rommel has never set foot in a restaurant before that one—not to run it, anyway."

"You're certain."

"My mother owned a country kitchen. I worked there for forty-two years before Mamma sold and retired to Florida. That man wouldn't know fine dining from a bologna sandwich."

"So what do you think is going on?"

"I don't know, but you can bet he's up to no good. Do you think he took that girl?"

"I don't know," Holt said, "but I'll be watching him closely."

"Be careful with that," Ms. Maude said. "He's got cunning. He plays all smooth and mannered, but I can see the wheels turning in the back of his eyes. The man's always looking for an angle—a weakness he can exploit."

"What's he got on Lorraine?"

"She's a lonely older woman who was married to a serial cheater. That's all a smooth talker like Rommel needs to get in the door. Some women don't listen to their instincts. They always pay for it in the end."

"Do you have any idea where he came from? If he has family around?"

"Not that I've ever heard of. Seemed like he just appeared one day after Walter Senior died and never left. I asked around back then, but no one seemed to know much about him. After a while, he became old news and people stopped asking."

Alex looked over at him and frowned. "I think it's time someone finds out exactly who Martin Rommel is and why he's in Vodoun."

HOLT PEERED OUT THE kitchen window of Sarah's home into the stormy night. Alex stepped up beside him and looked out into the inky blackness that the porch light failed miserably in illuminating.

"See anything?" she asked.

"Unless there was something to see six inches from the window, I'm not going to see a thing." He released the curtain and it slid back over the window. "Habit, I guess."

Alex nodded. "I just finished looking out the front window."

"There's a state trooper posted in a car across

the street. No one's coming in the front of the house."

"I know, but I have this feeling that someone's watching."

"Someone *is* watching—the state trooper."

Alex sighed. "You know what I mean."

Holt nodded. He'd had the same feeling all day, even though he'd found no evidence of a tail since the car incident that morning. Still, tailing wasn't necessary when everyone in Vodoun knew where Sarah lived. With the rental car parked out front, all it would take was a drive around the block to know exactly where they were.

"Did you find anything on Rommel?" Alex asked. Holt had dropped her off at Sarah's and went straight to the sheriff's department after their conversation with Ms. Maude, hoping to fill in the blanks on Lorraine's "business associate."

"Not a thing, and that's not a good sign. There's only three types of people who don't leave a trace on the internet—those who live as hermits, those who intentionally live off-radar or those who started as one person and are now masquerading as another."

"But surely there's something."

"Nothing. Not even a driver's license."

"Are you going to tell Lorraine?"

"No. I'm going to find a way to get a fingerprint first. You can change your look and identity, but prints always remain the same. If Rommel's gone to this much trouble to hide his identity, likely he'll have a record. If I go to Lorraine without proof, she won't believe me, and she'll warn him."

"Lorraine always was too stubborn for her own good."

He nodded. "I talked to Mathilde's doctor. He's releasing her tomorrow at noon."

"Are you going to arrest her?"

"I don't have any reason to believe she had anything to do with this. Certainly she didn't run our car off the road today or shoot someone in that alley."

"But Bobby's body was dumped somewhere near the island."

"I think someone is using Mathilde as a scapegoat. Someone who knows what happened years ago."

"You think they planted the barrette, too?"

"If someone were trying to frame her, it would fit."

"But it doesn't make sense, Holt. They cleaned out Bobby's place after they killed him to make it look like he's the one that took Erika. Why plant evidence on the island?"

"Yes, but dumping the body near the island

may have been a way to hedge their bets just in case it was discovered. That and the barrette."

"I guess that could be, but the biggest question still isn't answered—why kidnap Erika in the first place? She's just a little girl. Do you actually believe there's an organized gang of pedophiles kidnapping little girls then committing multiple murders to hide it all?"

Holt blew out a breath. "No, but I can't come up with a single idea that works."

Alex slapped her hand against the top of the couch. "It's all so maddening. There has to be logic behind this on some level, but yet all we find is more questions. Erika is still out there going through God knows what while Sarah slowly goes off the deep end. And we sit here in this house with armed guards and don't have even one idea about how to fix all this."

Tears welled up in her eyes and Holt stepped over to her and wrapped his arms around her. "We're going to figure it out," he whispered. "I promise you I will not rest until we find Erika."

"I won't rest, either." Alex held on to him for a bit then released him and swiped her hand across her cheek. "What are you going to do about Mathilde, then? Finding Bobby's leg may have put her in danger."

"If Mathilde knew anything that could help us, we already had an opportunity to get it out of her at the hospital. Any threat she posed for the killer has already been exposed. If he goes after Mathilde, it would change her status from suspect to victim as far as the killer knows."

"What about the barrette? If we can get Mathilde onto the island for the full moon tomorrow night and you give her back the barrette, she may be able to tell us where Erika is."

He stared. "You can't possibly believe that."

Alex threw her hands up in the air and flopped down on the couch. "I don't know what I believe anymore. If there's a logical explanation for everything, then what's yours for the crows or the doll?"

Holt walked over to the couch and took a seat beside her. "Just because I don't have one doesn't mean there isn't one. But the last thing we need is for you to start believing in curses and spooks and magic."

"Why? It's the only thing we haven't tried, and we're probably the last people in the parish to buy into it. Maybe that's the problem."

Holt blew out a breath. "I can't believe we're even having this conversation. What's going on, Alex? Why are you suddenly willing to believe in the old ways? Mathilde Tregre is a scared old woman who was in the wrong place at the wrong time."

"No. Mathilde Tregre is much more than a

scared old woman." Her mind flashed back to that day…to what she and Sarah saw.

Holt took her hand and squeezed. "Tell me why you say that," he said softly.

Chapter Fifteen

Alex knew it was time. Time to free herself of something she'd carried around for far too many years. Something she'd never been able to come to terms with. If anyone could help her put things in perspective, it would be Holt.

"Sarah and I weren't supposed to go to the island, but you know how Sarah is. She nagged and wheedled and made it sound like an adventure, until I couldn't say no."

Holt nodded. Sarah's tenacity was a well-known fact among her family and friends.

"We told her mom we were going to a friend's house to play, but instead we snuck out to old man LeBlanc's cabin and took his boat."

Holt smiled. "You stole a boat?"

"We brought it back, and besides, he was on vacation and not using it, anyway. I prefer 'borrowed.'"

"Most criminals do."

"Well, presumed criminal acts aside, we

took the boat into the swamp. Jenny Breaux had lifted a map to the island from her brother's room weeks before, and we'd made a copy. It was fun at the time—like finding a treasure map. I guess I never really thought Sarah would want to go or that she'd get me to agree to it, but as usual she managed."

"Was the map correct?"

"More or less. The water was low that summer, and some of the channels that were marked on the map were no longer there, but we managed to work our way around to the same points on the map.

"I remember it like it was yesterday," she continued. "We rounded that last corner and the island was right there in front of us. A cold chill ran over me when I saw the dolls, just like it did when we pulled up to the island the other day. I tried to get Sarah to turn around, but there was no stopping her."

"So you docked?"

"Yes. The pier was in decent shape then, so we tied the boat off and climbed out. I tried not to look at the dolls as we ran down the pier and onto the bank, but I could feel their eyes on me."

"You know they're just toys. I agree that they look creepy, but they can't hurt you."

Alex shook her head. "There's something

about them. Something that doesn't feel right. And why are they there? There's tons of legends and rumor and speculation, but no one knows why Mathilde's family started putting the dolls around the island. Most people believe it's to ward off spirits."

"More likely, it's to ward off anyone nosy enough to want to poke around."

"If that's the case, then I guess it's worked for the most part." Alex paused for a moment, trying to collect her thoughts before she told the next part of the story. "It was starting to cloud up by the time we docked. I was afraid we'd get caught in a storm, but Sarah promised if I'd spend ten minutes looking around, that she'd leave."

She stared at the wall for a moment, that long-ago day running through her mind like a film reel. "The path to the cabin was wider then and easily passable, or maybe it was a different path than the one that's there now. Either way, we hurried down it and crouched in the bushes at the edge of the clearing.

"We could hear someone inside moaning, then there was a blood-curdling scream—like someone being murdered. I wanted to run, but I was frozen in place. I heard Sarah suck in a breath that she never blew out. Then the swamp went completely silent, and the only thing I heard was the sound of my own heartbeat—like a bass drum booming so hard it made my chest hurt."

Holt squeezed her hand.

"I finally got control of myself and was just about to pull on Sarah to leave when Mathilde came out of the cabin. She was younger then, but her hair was already turning silver."

She took a breath and slowly blew it out. "She was dragging a body behind her."

Holt sat upright on the couch and stared. "A human body?"

"Yes. It was wrapped in a blanket that she was pulling, but one arm was hanging out, dragging along in the dirt." Alex crossed her arms in front of chest and shuddered. "When she stopped behind the cabin, I realized there was a fresh grave."

"She buried the body behind her cabin?"

Alex nodded. "It took her a bit to drag it into the hole, but she managed. Then she picked up a burlap bag that was sitting next to the hole and pulled out a doll—the same doll that Sarah found in Erika's room."

"You're certain it was the same?"

"Positive. Mathilde held the doll up and did some sort of chant, then dropped the doll into the grave with the body. Then she pulled a square piece of wood laying next to the grave, into the hole."

"The top to a homemade casket?"

"That's what it looked like. She shoved a reed in the middle of the hole and it stood up straight out of the grave. Then she started shoveling dirt onto the grave."

"You waited there the entire time?"

"Yes, and it felt like forever, but looking back, it couldn't have been that long. I don't think the hole was very deep."

Holt shook his head. "No wonder you were scared."

"Oh, that's not the scary part. Not at all."

Holt stared. "Then what is?"

"When she finished covering the grave, she dropped a rock with a piece of string tied around it down the reed. Then she tied a bell to the other end of the string and attached it to the top of the reed. I wanted to run but I knew she'd hear us if we made a run for it. We crouched there, not moving, barely breathing and prayed that she went back inside the cabin so we could get away."

"That is a situation most adults couldn't have handled. I can't imagine how you and Sarah managed...."

"I guess we had a guardian angel watching over us. I thought once she finished the grave, she'd leave, but instead, she sat on an old stump next to the grave. She was waiting for something. I could feel it."

Alex looked Holt directly in the eyes. "And then the bell started to ring."

Holt's eyes widened. "Maybe the wind—"

"There wasn't a breath of air, and besides, I could see the string moving down the reed... tight, like it was being pulled.

"Mathilde started removing the dirt from the grave, and pulled the top off the coffin." Alex rose from the couch and paced once across the living room and came back to stand in front of Holt.

"Then she helped the dead person climb out of the grave."

Holt jumped up off the couch and stared at her. "No way!"

"I swear on everything that's holy, an old woman climbed out of that grave, clutching that creepy doll."

"But that's impossible."

"You think I don't know that? Why do you think I've never told anyone what we saw? I'm a psychiatrist. People didn't believe you when you claimed to see a very real human leaving your house after your father's murder. What in the world would people think if I spread that story around?"

He sighed. "They'd think you were crazy."

"Exactly, and that's a chance I'm just not going to take. I know what I saw. Yes, I was scared half to death, but it was broad daylight and I had a clear, reasonably close view. That woman came back from the dead."

Holt ran one hand through his hair and flopped back down on the couch. "I don't even know what to say. That's the most outlandish thing I've ever heard."

Alex bit her lower lip and sat beside him. "But you believe me?"

He looked her straight in the eye. "Of course I believe you."

"But you think there has to be a logical explanation."

"Don't you?"

She blew out a breath and stared at the wall for a minute. "I used to think so, and I wanted one."

"But you don't now?"

"I don't know." She looked back at Holt. "What if Mathilde does have some sort of power that can't be explained by science? Then maybe tomorrow night, during the full moon, she can find Erika."

Holt studied her for a couple of seconds, and she could tell he wanted to discount her suggestion, to tell her she was grasping at straws, but empathy must have won out because instead he wrapped his arms around her and held her close.

"If you want to let her try," he said, "I'll make it happen."

THE KILLER SLID BEHIND the hedges, looking down the street at Sarah's house. Every blind was drawn, but he knew they were in there, wondering when he would strike next. He looked at the unmarked trooper parked across the street. Did they really think he was so foolish that he didn't recognize a cop when he saw one?

He hadn't managed all these years to fly below law enforcement radar by being a fool. And now, he was poised to spend the rest of his life in the comfort he deserved.

And for that, he'd do anything required.

His boss was getting anxious and so was he. The fake sheriff and nosy broad had come too close for comfort, and he was going to have to eliminate that threat, as well. He just needed a way to cast the blame on someone else.

Once the old woman was back on the island, he'd be able to set everything in motion.

ALEX POURED TWO CUPS of coffee and carried them to the breakfast table where Sarah sat.

Holt had left for New Orleans intending to check on his truck and then pick up Mathilde to bring her back to Vodoun. After he had her review her statement and look at some pictures at the sheriff's station, they were going to take her back to the island. Holt wanted to search for any evidence that might tell them more about Bobby's murder or Erika's location, and then they'd wait for the sun to go down and the full moon to rise so that Mathilde could do a reading.

Sarah poured sugar into her coffee and stirred as Alex took a seat across from her. "You're letting me drink coffee?"

"At this point, a little caffeine is the least of our problems."

"This is all so surreal," Sarah said. "If you'd told me before today that all this would be happening to me, I'd say you were crazy."

"It's all quite unbelievable, but unfortunately, all very real."

Sarah sniffed and rubbed her nose with her finger. Her eyes were still puffy and red from crying, and the circles underneath grew darker with each day that passed. "I still can't believe Bobby's gone, you know? I know I filed for divorce, but I think I always hoped he'd get his head on straight and we could work things out."

Alex reached across the table and squeezed Sarah's hand. "I know. I always hoped so, too."

"I just don't understand what's happening."

"Neither do I, but we're going to figure it all out. I promise."

Sarah stared at her for a moment, then nodded. "I know you will. I believe in you...and Holt." She opened her mouth to speak again then hesitated.

Finally, she said, "Do you really think the witch woman can use magic to determine where Erika is?"

Alex didn't have any idea what she thought at this point, but the hopeful sound in Sarah's voice tugged so hard at her heart that she couldn't bring herself to tell her cousin that it might all be a big waste of time. "I hope so," she said finally.

"What we saw when we were kids...that was real, right?"

"It was real. I can't say it was magic or voodoo, but what we saw did happen. That much I'm sure of."

Sarah nodded. "How are you and Holt getting along?"

"Fine. I mean, he's still as hard-headed and closed off as before, but he's doing everything he can to find Erika. He's a good investigator."

"You still love him."

Alex sat her cup of coffee down and stared at her cousin. "Certainly, seeing him again and working so closely with him has brought back memories, but I don't…" Even though the words were right there, in her mind and on the tip of her tongue, she couldn't bring herself to say them.

"Love him?" Sarah gave her a sympathetic look. "You can keep telling *yourself* that, but you made a promise a long time ago to never lie to me."

Alex sighed. "Yes, I love him. I knew the moment I saw him standing in your house that I'd never stopped. But what difference does that make? Holt's changed in a lot of ways, but not in the ones that make for a good relationship."

"Maybe he just needs more time."

"He's had ten years. If he doesn't know what he wants by now, then he's a really poor bet for me. If it wasn't for Erika's kidnapping, I wouldn't even have known he was in Vodoun. That tells me all I need to know."

"Oh, honey." Sarah sighed. "You two are the most stubborn people I know. Almost as bad as me. Promise me that you won't let pride get in the way if it's possible for you and Holt to have a future."

"Pride? I gave up on pride ten years ago when I begged him not to leave. This isn't pride. It's survival."

HOLT PARKED IN FRONT of the sheriff's department, and went to open the car door for Mathilde. The old woman frowned as he pulled her door open and waved him away when he extended his hand.

"I'm not that injured or that old," she said. "Let's get this over with. I want to get back to my island. I'm not right when I'm not on my land."

Holt wasn't sure Mathilde was "right" when she was on her land, either, but it didn't seem like the sort of assessment he should share with her, especially as she'd been complaining all the way from New Orleans to Vodoun about being "held hostage" for so long by the hospital. His conversation with his uncle that morning on the way to New Orleans had been equally as pleasant.

Despite his uncle's shock and discomfort at Bobby's death, he didn't think it was a good use of "department resources" to play taxi driver, especially when Jasper was still holding on to the idea that Mathilde was the perpetrator. He was equally resistant to the idea that anything more could be found by searching the island.

Holt could only imagine what sort of outrage he'd have experienced if he'd told the man Alex's plan for using voodoo to locate Erika.

He pushed all that out of his mind and held open the front door of the sheriff's department for Mathilde to enter. She glared at him as she walked past.

"Did you find out who that leg belonged to with all that fancy machinery used these days?"

"Yes. It belonged to the missing girl's father."

Mathilde frowned. "That's not good."

"No. It's not, and it's why we need to move fast and why I'm willing to try anything at this point to find Erika."

Holt pointed her to a chair in front of his desk and handed her a picture of the dead man from the alley that he'd taken in the hospital morgue. "Have you ever seen this man before?"

Mathilde studied the picture for a couple of seconds, then shook her head. "Is he the man who took the girl?"

"We think so, and we think he's the man who killed her father and dumped the body."

"He's dead?"

"Yes, but he wasn't working alone. Someone else was giving the order. That man shot this one and got away, but I overheard them talking about dumping the body." Holt pulled out a photo of Martin Rommel. "What about this man?"

Mathilde gave him a disgusted look. "I seen him last time I came to Vodoun for supplies. Catting around with that fancy blond bitch. Young enough to be her son, but she don't act like a mother toward him. It's indecent, is what it is."

"Have you seen him anywhere near the island?"

"I ain't seem him or the bitch, or I'd shoot them both. She's the one that sent the police after me the first time, with all her tales of the evil witch in the swamp. Made a lot of trouble for me for a lot of years. I got nothing for her or her man."

Disappointed, Holt placed the pictures back on the desk and handed her the statement he'd typed up based on the recording he'd made in the hospital. Mathilde looked at the papers, but didn't make a move to take them. Then it hit him.

"You can't read," he said.

"Ain't no one in my family ever needed to. I ain't no different."

"I'll just read it to you, then."

Mathilde's eyes narrowed. "How do I know you won't lie about what's on there?"

"Why would I do that?"

"To get me to sign something saying I took that girl and fed her daddy to the gator."

"Ms. Tregre, I don't think you took the girl, and I don't think you took those girls years ago. I don't know what's going on in this town, but I'm going to find out."

Mathilde stared at him, studying his face. He must have passed her test, because finally she nodded. "Read your report, then. Daylight's a-wasting."

THREE HOURS LATER, Holt, Mathilde and Alex docked on the island. Alex exited the boat and offered her hand to Mathilde, but the old woman waved her away and climbed out of the boat, knee-deep in water, then sloshed through the murky water and climbed onto the bank.

Alex looked over at Holt, who shrugged. She'd already sensed that Holt's morning with Mathilde hadn't been overly pleasant, and clearly the crotchety old woman was well beyond her limits of dealing with people. She hoped Mathilde was physically able to conduct a search of the island with them.

They'd left Vodoun from Holt's cabin rather than the dock, trying to ensure they weren't followed to the island. Holt had put a tail on Rommel that morning, just in case the man was involved, but he'd left Lorraine's house that morning, gone straight to the restaurant and was still there when they left Holt's cabin. With no fear of a tail, they'd taken off from Holt's cabin and used the tiny, rarely used channels to access the island, reducing the chance of being seen by fishermen.

As Alex turned to follow Mathilde up the bank, she hit a doll on one of the old posts from the dilapidated dock and it fell in the water.

"Oh!" Alex reached down for the doll, then froze. It was the same doll. The doll that Erika had. The doll that she and Sarah had seen that day.

Mathilde stopped and turned to see what had made her cry out. The old woman studied her for a moment, then walked over and retrieved the doll from the bayou.

"Do the dolls bother you?" Mathilde asked.

"Yes," Alex replied, seeing no reason to lie. "I find them macabre."

Mathilde nodded. "I figure most people do, but then it keeps people away, so there's that."

"Did you put them all here? And if so, why?"

"My mama started it. Started it with this doll. She bought two of 'em. One was mine. One was my twin sister's. Mama traded herbs in town to get them for our birthday. They were the first new things we'd ever seen, much less owned. Oh, how Adelaide loved that doll."

Mathilde looked off down the bayou, and Alex knew she was remembering the past.

"Don't get me wrong," Mathilde said, "I loved the doll, too, but not like Adelaide. That's why Mama buried her with it when she died. Only seven years old, and even though Mama had the power, there wasn't nothing she could do to save Adelaide."

"What happened to her?"

"We were playing in our pirogue on the other side of the island—where we shouldn't have been. Adelaide was rocking the pirogue back and forth to scare me as I ain't that keen a swimmer. She finally succeeded in flipping it over, but we was right over a sunken boat. It had probably been in that channel for a decade, decaying and rusting.

"Adelaide fell right on a piece of rusted metal. Cut her leg all up the inside. It was all I could do to get her to shore, then I ran to get Mama. But she was already dead by the time we got back. Mama said too much life had left her body."

Likely Adelaide had severed her femoral artery. She wouldn't have stood a chance of survival this far away from a medical facility. "I'm very sorry," Alex said.

"Thank you," Mathilde said. "Mama lost a piece of her mind that day. A piece she never gained back. Whenever she could manage the extra, she bought a doll and placed it on the bank, facing the water. Sometimes she found them at flea markets or in Dumpsters. She brought them all to the island. That way, Adelaide had all the dolls she could love."

Mathilde looked down at the doll. "This one was mine—the matching one to Adelaide's. I put it up here the day we buried her and have only touched it one time since. Every year, on the day of Adelaide's death, I put another doll out."

Alex felt her heart clench for the mother and the sister, who'd spent so many years mourning the loss of a young life taken tragically. "I think that's a beautiful sentiment, Mathilde. It makes me see the dolls differently now."

"Others don't see it the same. Some claim the dolls is here to draw children to the island. Some say that's why I took those girls back years ago—to replace my dead sister, but I would never harm a child."

"Of course not."

Mathilde gave her a brief nod. "Well, we got another girl waiting to be found. We best get on with it."

Alex followed Mathilde up the path to her cabin, her mind dwelling on the heartbreaking story the old woman had just told. So many rumors and lies had circled around the island and the dolls for so many years, and now it all seemed to be crashing down, at least in Alex's mind. She heard Holt fall in place behind her and felt his hand on her shoulder as he gave it a gentle squeeze.

He'd been moved by Mathilde's story, as well. She'd seen the sympathy and just a touch of pain on his face. The little boy who'd lost so much at an early age had gone to war and lost even more. No wonder he was afraid to commit. Still, understanding the why didn't make it hurt any less.

She blew out a breath and picked up her pace to match Mathilde's. They had to find Erika. Alex wouldn't be able to live with herself if Sarah went the same way as Holt—afraid to love anything for fear of losing it.

When they reached Mathilde's cabin, the old woman stalked inside and shook her head at the glass from the jar that had fallen days before. "Is that your mess?" she asked.

"I'm sorry," Alex said. "The jar fell in front of us as we were leaving."

Mathilde frowned. "It fell? You didn't bump anything or jostle the door?"

"No. We hadn't even reached the door yet when it fell."

Mathilde nodded. "It's an omen. If you hadn't

found the barrette, you might not have searched the island and wouldn't have saved me from the gator. I'm supposed to help you find the girl, otherwise the broken jar wouldn't have set you on the path."

Mathilde opened a jar of dried herbs and put a pinch of them under her tongue. "Coulda been healed two days ago if I had my herbs." She exited the cabin and waved at them to follow. "You two gonna hafta move faster to keep up with me."

Holt shook his head in admiration. "I had men in my troop with less fortitude," he said before following her out of the cabin.

Alex followed them into the swamp, hoping Mathilde's skill matched her attitude.

Chapter Sixteen

Holt recognized the path that he followed Mathilde on. "This is the path to where we found you, right?"

"Yeah," Mathilde said. "I figured you'd want to start there, since that's where you found the leg. That's the same bank I found the barrette on."

Holt felt his heart clench, and he gave a silent plea that Erika had not met the same fate as her father. "Could you tell if the barrette had been in the water or dropped on land?"

Mathilde scrunched her forehead as she pushed through the brush. "Not sure, really. It was on the edge of the bank, but the tide was high. Coulda washed up there. Coulda been dropped there. Wasn't a bit of rust on it, but if it was only dropped this week, wasn't long enough for the water to do its job."

Holt nodded. He'd figured that was the case, but verification was always a good thing. It narrowed options. "Did you recognize the alligator that attacked you?"

"Yep. I call him Grand. The bayous around the island has been his territory for years. He kills any bulls that tries to move in."

It wasn't the answer Holt hoped for. A bull that aggressive would see any encroachment, by animal or man, as a threat to his territory. Based on the conversation he'd overheard with the killer, he figured Bobby was already dead when the killer dumped the body in the bayou. So either the body had washed up on shore, or more likely, the alligator had retrieved it from the bottom and carried it onshore for a snack.

Even though it was a gruesome discovery, they'd been lucky to find it, or they might never have known for certain that Bobby Rhonaldo was dead. The killers hadn't mentioned Erika's status at all during their conversation in the alley, but then, that conversation had been fairly short given that the one in charge had murdered his flunky.

It took them forty-five minutes to arrive back at the site of the alligator attack. Mathilde checked the bank for any sign of Grand, then stepped right up to the water and scanned the bayou in front of them.

"You can come at this side of the island by a number of channels," Mathilde said. "If the

body was dumped, it's likely it was out there."
She pointed to a stretch of bayou directly in
front of them. "That part's fairly deep com-
pared to others, and I've never seen it below the
tide line. Your killer probably thought whatever
he put there was gone forever."

"I guess he wasn't counting on Grand."

"No." Mathilde pointed to a patch of marsh
grass just off to the left of the clearing. "Right
there's where I found the barrette. Caught my
attention immediately. Not supposed to be any
little girls out in the swamp, which is why I
took it with me intending to do a reading. Kids
ain't got the skill to survive out here like Mama
taught me."

"You never saw or heard a boat?"

Mathilde shook her head. "But I wasn't on
this side of the island until the day you found
me. I hear the echo of boat engines sometimes,
but here in the swamp, they carry for miles. I
have no way of knowing if I heard the boat that
dumped the body, and even if I did, I wouldn't
be able to give you a time as that's not something I pay mind to."

Holt nodded. "If someone were going to hide
the girl on this island, where would they do it?"

"I've got a shack on the south side that I keep
in good enough shape to spend a night or two
for checking my trout lines. But it's pretty well

hidden. Someone would have to know the island well enough to find it. Ain't no one going to happen upon it unless they was out here looking for something."

"How far away is it?"

"'Bout as long as the walk here if you stick to the bank. A little less if you cut straight through."

"Let's stick to the bank for now," Holt said. "Just in case there's something to find."

Mathilde stepped through a patch of marsh grass to the right of them. "This way."

The trip to the shack took a little less than forty-five minutes but seemed longer, as there was no trail along the bank. The terrain shifted from mud to marsh grass every few feet and some sections were so dense with growth that they had to move farther into the swamp to pass around. Holt noticed he wasn't the only person keeping an eye on every step and on the water. No one wanted to have another run-in with Grand.

The word *shack* was probably a stretch for the dilapidated structure of driftwood that stood in a tiny clearing, but then, Mathilde's needs were far less than that of the average person. Likely, she used the shack only to protect her from the worst of the weather and night creatures out here in the swamp.

He poked his head inside and saw a layer of thick dust on a handmade table. "Doesn't look like anyone's been here."

Mathilde looked inside the shack, then walked the perimeter. "I don't see no signs of recent passage, except for the usual swamp creatures. No man's walked here in a while or it would show, especially with the storms we've had."

"I agree," Holt said. He looked over at Alex, who nodded, the disappointment and fear clearly evident in her expression. The more defeated she became, the more Holt worried about her and Sarah and how they'd cope if things turned out badly.

Alex looked at her watch, then up at the dark clouds swirling above them. "There's another storm in the forecast. It will get dark early. Maybe we should head back to the cabin to get ready for tonight."

Mathilde looked up at the black clouds. "Another omen. Something dark besides them clouds has come over this town…over my island. Skies looked the same thirty-six years ago. I aim to expose everything tonight and get rid of them clouds forever."

Mathilde headed toward a barely visible trail behind the shack, Alex trailing behind her. Holt looked up at the menacing sky. It didn't look any different than any other storm the gulf produced. But it felt different.

Like something was coming.

THE KILLER PULLED HIS BOAT UP the bank of the island some distance from the old dock. He hoped to find the fake sheriff and the woman before the storm hit. Bad enough, he had to come out into the swamp to finish this business, but their death on the island still offered the best cover for all involved.

He crept around the edge of the bank until he had a clear view of the dock. The sheriff's department's boat was there, just as the boss had suspected it would be. The fake sheriff and the woman would be there, with the old lady. It was almost a shame to kill the old lady. She'd kept to herself, living off the land all these years, and now she was caught in the middle of something she knew nothing about.

But first, he had to do a sweep of the island and make sure that idiot hadn't left any other evidence of their passing. If he'd handled the job with the body correctly, it would never have surfaced. Stealing it from the lab had been an excellent idea, but he'd been too late. Now that the cops knew Bobby was dead, they'd start looking for other answers. The witch woman was the answer his boss wanted them to rest on.

The killer hoped that tonight this entire ordeal would be over and he could get back to his real business, but even if things turned out badly, he had no problem disappearing. His past was concealed under a different name. His new identity was spotless. So spotless he could disappear and wouldn't leave a single trace except for people's word.

Not that disappearing was part of his plan anytime soon. He needed a couple more years for his plan to come off in full force. All he had to do was make sure no one ever found the girl, and the key to the throne was his.

ALEX WATCHED IN FASCINATION as Mathilde prepared for the night's reading. First she began to boil bayou water, adding some leaves that smelled like a combination of garlic and spearmint. After allowing the water to boil for a bit, she scooped the leaves out of the pot and placed them in a bowl of clean water she'd set in the center of her table. Steam rose off the leaves as they hit the cold water, and Mathilde intently watched the steam.

Once the steam dissipated, she turned her attention to the leaves in the bowl, staring down at them as if she were reading a book. That's when Alex realized she was reading—reading the leaves. Alex looked over at Holt, who stood in the corner quietly observing everything. He raised his eyebrows, suggesting he wasn't quite sure what to make of the display, either.

Finally, Mathilde looked up at Alex. "The steam rose straight with no swirls. That means the spirits are open to us. We'll get a good reading tonight."

"And the leaves?" Alex asked.

Mathilde frowned. "I get betrayal and old sins and death, but it's impossible to know if that applies to the child or not. The leaves sank fast, meaning either the answers you seek will become buried as they have in the past or that the time for the lies has ended and they will fade from this world."

"So we'll either get an answer or go away with absolutely no answer," Alex said. "That doesn't seem very helpful."

"No," Mathilde agreed. "There seems to be a lot of confusion around the happenings. I think there's more going on here than just the missing girl."

"That makes two of us," Holt said.

Mathilde pointed to a shelf behind Alex. "Hand me that jar with the brown twigs in it. I might get more reading the twigs."

Alex turned to the shelf and located the jar Mathilde wanted, but as she pulled it off, a flash of silver behind the jar caught her eye. It was the bell. The bell that a dead woman had rang.

Alex sucked in a breath and froze. Instantly, she was taken back to that day where she was a terrified little girl.

"Can't you find it?" Mathilde asked and walked up beside her. She reached for the jar, but couldn't pull it out of Alex's grip. "Let go of the jar."

"Alex," Holt said, coming up to stand on the other side of her. "What's wrong?"

"The bell," she said. "That's the bell the dead woman rang."

Mathilde stared at her. "It was you. I always knew someone was there watching. Mama said it was my imagination, but I could feel your eyes on me. You weren't alone, though, were you?"

Alex looked at her in amazement. "No, my cousin was with me. The mother of the missing child."

Mathilde nodded. "That's the connection I've been feeling. I couldn't put my finger on it before, but I knew you and that missing girl was tied to the island some way."

"She came back from the dead. We saw it happen."

Mathilde shook her head. "Not exactly. What you saw was a rebirth."

"What is a rebirth?" Holt asked.

"Mama took the potion—the special one that brings your body almost to a stop. Once her body slowed, I buried her as she'd instructed me to. When the potion wore off, she woke up and rang the bell so's I could dig her up."

"But why?" Alex asked. "Why in the world would she want to be buried alive?"

"'Cause a rebirth on the first day of the full moon brings great power. Mama felt with more power, she'd be able to speak directly to Adelaide at the height of the full moon."

"She wasn't dead," Alex said, trying to absorb it all.

"No. She was just in a state of limbo between the spirit world and this one, drawing on their power."

"But the scream…"

Mathilde nodded. "Mama said the potion burned like fire once it hit your stomach. That scream was her way of releasing the pain from her body."

"Have you ever been rebirthed?" Holt asked Mathilde.

Mathilde shot him a derisive look. "'Course not. Who the hell would have buried me and dug me up?" She waved a hand at him. "You city folk have forgotten how to think."

Alex smiled and picked up the silver bell,

turning it over in her hands. It felt as if a giant weight had been lifted from her body, and she couldn't wait to tell Sarah. Hopefully, her conversation with Sarah would include news on Erika. It was a stretch for her to buy into Mathilde's "powers," but too many odd things had happened for her to ignore. And at the moment, they had no clue where Erika was. Alex was tilting over into desperation.

She handed Mathilde the sticks and placed the silver bell back on the shelf. Maybe things would be revealed tonight as they had been this evening. Maybe all the answers they were looking for would start to unfold tonight.

Maybe.

MATHILDE SET A MAKESHIFT ALTAR at the edge of the bank near the old dock. On top of it, she placed the bowl she'd used for reading leaves and a jar of something she'd brewed that smelled awful and had made Alex's eyes burn so badly she'd left the cabin. Two black candles completed the assortment of objects.

Mathilde had ditched her ragged jeans and T-shirt and replaced them with a black robe. Her silver hair seemed to glow in the dark as she arranged the items on the altar and checked the moon as it rose above the tree line.

"Only a few minutes more," Mathilde said.

"When the moonlight reaches the altar, I can begin."

Alex watched nervously as the moonlight crept up the bank, inching toward the altar. The predicted storm was brewing overhead, and if it came up before Mathilde could do the reading, the dark clouds could completely block the moonlight, making the reading impossible.

Holt eased beside her and took her hand in his and squeezed. She knew he didn't believe and was afraid of her disappointment if they found nothing to help find Erika. She also knew he was frustrated that he'd been unable to do more.

Mathilde pulled a box of matches from her pocket and lit the candles, placing them on each side of the bowl. The moonlight crept up the side of the altar, and she poured the liquid into the bowl then raised her arms toward the sky. As the moonlight inched into the bowl, she began chanting, first low and soft and increasing in volume as she continued.

Alex felt a pain in her chest and realized she was holding her breath. The air left her body in a whoosh and for a moment, she was afraid the sound would disturb the ceremony, but Mathilde was looking skyward, her eyes clenched and voice loud and clear. Alex remembered a little of the Creole language from her childhood and could make out the words *answers*, *child*, *mother* and *offering*.

Mathilde had a handmade necklace in her pocket that she was going to offer to the spirits in exchange for information on Erika. When the moonlight filled the bowl, she pulled out the necklace and placed it next to the bowl, then placed Erika's barrette on top of the liquid.

Alex glanced at the sky, growing more anxious as the dark clouds swirled closer and closer to the moon. When Mathilde began to chant again, a flash of lightning tore right overhead and Alex jumped. The static electricity in the air made Mathilde's hair stand on end like glowing silver strands in the moonlight, but even the booming thunder that followed didn't cause her to pause.

Suddenly, Mathilde stopped chanting and stared down at the bowl, then watched the smoke from the candles as it whipped away in the stormy sky. "The child is close. So is the person who took her. The child's in a dark place below the ground. She's scared and cries for her mama."

Mathilde looked over at them. "The person you seek has a dark heart. The spirits cannot determine the intent for the child, but it's not good."

"Is she on the island?" Alex asked.

"No, and she's never been here. The barrette was placed here by the evil man to divert suspicion."

Suddenly, Mathilde froze, then pointed west. "Danger is coming. We must get to safety." She grabbed the necklace from the altar, then waved Holt and Alex toward the boat. "You must leave. He's coming."

Despite the incredulity of the situation, something in the woman's voice sent Holt into action. He pulled Alex toward the dock with one hand, while yanking the boat keys from his pocket with the other. Lightning flashed again, illuminating the bayou, and thunder rolled across the sky, echoing across the water.

"Hurry!" Mathilde yelled, as they ran for the dock.

"Too late." Martin Rommel stepped out from a patch of marsh grass just to the side of the dock, holding a nine-millimeter.

Chapter Seventeen

He leveled the gun at them and stood directly in the path to the boat. "That little show the witch put on was quite interesting. Not very revealing, but then that's the whole point of magic, right? Leaving everything open to interpretation so that you're always right."

"She knew you were here," Alex said.

"A little too late," Rommel said and motioned to Holt. "Remove your gun from your waist and toss it over here. Nice and slow, or your girlfriend takes a bullet to the head."

Alex saw the muscles in Holt's jaw clench as he removed his pistol and tossed it at Rommel's feet. She had Ms. Maude's pistol tucked in the back waistband of her jeans. If only Rommel didn't realize she was armed, they may have a chance.

"You too, honey," he directed Alex. "Slow and gentle—give me that nine-millimeter."

Deflated, she pulled the nine-millimeter

from her waistband and tossed it on the ground in front of Rommel, certain that they'd just lost their last chance at getting away.

"Is my niece still alive?" Alex asked, determined to know no matter the outcome.

"Yes."

"Why? Why would you kidnap a child? Are you some sort of pervert?"

Rommel gave her a disgusted look. "Of course not. She'll be sold to a Russian family next week, and will likely make a very beautiful slave."

"I guess even a murderer has standards," Holt said.

Rommel smiled. "You should know. After all, soldiers are merely killers with permission. It's all business, after all."

"Kidnapping little girls is hardly the same as fighting a war against terrorists," Alex said. "Only a person with no morals would compare the two."

"Morals?" Rommel laughed. "The last time I checked, morals didn't make one rich. My boss had a problem with your niece, so I eliminated the problem. It's a business transaction. That's all."

"What kind of person has a problem with a child?" Alex asked. "Your boss is a sick man."

"Most certainly, but the pay is extraordinary." Rommel waved his pistol at Mathilde. "Move over closer to the other two so I can get this over with. I don't feel like getting caught out here in the storm."

Mathilde didn't move and when Alex looked over, she realized the woman's eyes were closed and her lips were moving. Whether she was praying or chanting, Alex couldn't say, but all of a sudden, the wind picked up speed.

"Now!" Rommel yelled at Mathilde as dark clouds started moving over the moon.

The light in the clearing began to dissipate from the outside in, leaving a smaller and smaller area of light. Alex glanced over at Holt, so many things racing through her mind that she wished she could say, but the only thing that mattered now was staying alive. Holt gave her a barely imperceptible nod, and she knew he was thinking what she was. As soon as the light was gone, they were going to make a break for it.

Alex hoped Mathilde would come to the same conclusion, but the woman's eyes were clenched tight. Silently, she willed Mathilde to open her eyes before the slim opportunity they had to get away disappeared completely.

Suddenly, Mathilde opened her eyes and flung the necklace she held out into the bayou. That action was all it took to make Rommel fire, but at the same time, Mathilde dove into the deep brush of the swamp, seeming to defy her age and gravity with her leap.

Before Alex could even spin around to run, a giant surge of water rose from the bank and Grand launched from the bayou, grabbing Rommel in his giant jaws. Rommel screamed and pounded on the giant reptile with his hands, his gun lost during the attack. Alex watched in horror as the alligator shook the man back and forth and a loud crack echoed across the clearing. Rommel went limp and Alex knew his neck was broken. The alligator immediately backed into the water, dragging his prize down in the murky depths.

The sound of Mathilde thrashing about in the brush brought Alex out of her trance, and she and Holt hurried over to help the woman up. She had scratches on her face and hands from the brush, but Alex was relieved to see that she hadn't been shot.

"Are you all right?" Alex asked.

"I guess I'm not in as good a shape as I thought," Mathilde said ruefully, as Alex helped steady her, "but I'm alive. That's a sight better than I can say for him." She motioned to the bayou then looked over at Holt. "I thought you was checking up on him?"

"I am...was," Holt replied. "I had someone

watching him this morning. He was at the restaurant when we left."

"Then how'd he come to know where we were?"

"She's right," Alex said. "Rommel couldn't have followed us, so how did he know where we were? The only person I told was Sarah, and she wouldn't tell a soul."

"I ain't got no one to tell," Mathilde said, "and wouldn't have besides."

They both looked at Holt. "I only told the state trooper shadowing Rommel. If something happened, he needed to know we couldn't be reached."

"But he wouldn't tell anyone, would he?" Alex asked.

"He's not even from Vodoun," Holt said.

He frowned and stared out across the bayou, then his face contorted with rage. "But if Jasper called in, the trooper would have told him. He had no reason not to."

"You can't really think…" Alex gasped. "Someone above reproach."

"I don't know anything for certain, but you can bet we're going to find out." Holt ran to the boat and lifted the rope from the pylon.

"Are you okay here?" Alex asked Mathilde.

"Of course," Mathilde replied. "You go find

that little girl, and then you come back and tell me."

"I promise," Alex said.

HOLT THREW THE RENTAL CAR in drive and tore away from his cabin, tires spinning on the dirt road. He had no idea what he was going to say to his uncle, but he'd figure it out when he got there. His mind was still reeling from the revelation that Jasper had to be the source of the information. He hadn't yet come to grips with the fact that his uncle might actually be the guilty party, and even as little as he liked the man, he didn't want to believe him capable of all that had happened.

But it fit. His uncle would have known Rommel through his mother, and he wouldn't question the man's lack of identity if he was using him to carry out his own nefarious plans. But why? What could he possibly gain from kidnapping a child?

Holt could feel Alex's gaze on him, and he knew she was worried about what he'd do when they reached his uncle's house. If he could reassure her, he would, but he wasn't about to offer any promises he might not be able to keep. If Jasper was responsible for all this horror, Holt wasn't sure how he was going to react.

His uncle's house was only a couple of miles

from his cabin where they docked the boat, and he made the drive in no time, screeching to a stop in the driveway. The lights were on in the living room and he could see the television flickering through the open blinds. His uncle was slouched on a recliner in the corner. Could he really be so relaxed if he'd sent a man to kill them?

Before he could open the car door, Alex placed her hand on his arm. "Don't do anything rash."

"You mean like find out where the hell Erika is?"

Alex bit her lip. "No, I want to know where Erika is, I just don't want you to get in trouble doing it. Or shot. If your uncle was paying Rommel for his dirty work, he's not going down without a fight once he sees we're alive."

"That broken leg of his puts him at a disadvantage. I will try reasoning first, but one way or another, he's going to answer every question I ask."

Holt pushed the car door open and stalked to the front door. He pounded on the door, yelling out, "It's Holt. Open up."

"It's unlocked," Jasper yelled back.

"Be careful," Alex said. "He may have a gun."

Holt nodded then pushed the door open and stepped inside. His uncle didn't make an effort to move, and Holt was relieved to see that the only thing he clutched in his hand was a beer. He looked a little confused at Holt's presence but didn't seem surprised or alarmed. Surely, if he'd hired Rommel, he'd be shocked that they were standing in his living room.

"What in the world has got you ruffled this late at night?" Jasper asked.

"I ran into some problems on the island."

Jasper shook his head. "I told you that woman was crazy. Floored me when that trooper told me you were taking her back there. The sheriff's department is not a taxi service. Any of the fishermen could have dropped her off."

"It wasn't Mathilde that was the problem. It was Martin Rommel."

Sheriff Conroy frowned, clearly confused. "What does Rommel have to do with any of it?"

Holt stared directly at his uncle, watching him closely before he said, "He tried to kill us tonight on the island."

Jasper sat straight up in his chair, the look of shock on his face so genuine that Holt didn't believe he was faking.

"What?"

"Rommel showed up and said he worked for the person who had Erika kidnapped. He said his 'boss' insisted that Alex and I had to die.

Apparently, we were getting too close in our investigation."

Jasper's jaw dropped and he looked back and forth from Alex to Holt, clearly waiting for the punch line of what had to be the world's worst joke. "You're not kidding," he said finally. "My god, you're not kidding."

"You knew nothing about this."

"No! How could you even think—"

"Then who did you tell? You called looking for me, and the state trooper told you that Alex and I were taking Mathilde back to the island, right?"

"Yes, but I don't see—"

"That makes you the only other person besides Sarah who knew where we were. Rommel didn't find us by luck, and he didn't follow us out there. I made sure of that. So who did you tell?"

The blood rushed from Jasper's face and he shook his head. "No…it's not possible. She couldn't…you must be wrong."

"Lorraine," Alex said. "He told his mother." She grabbed Holt's sleeve. "Mathilde said Erika was in a dark place below ground."

Holt immediately caught on. "Lorraine has a basement."

Jasper's expression grew angry. "If you're

accusing my mother of kidnapping that child, you better have some proof."

"You just gave it to me. Get out of that chair. You're going with me to search your mother's house for Erika."

"You don't have a warrant."

"You think I care about a warrant!" Holt glared at Jasper, daring him to launch even one more argument. "Now, get out of that chair and in my car. I'm not about to give you an opportunity to call and warn her that we're coming."

Apparently, Jasper decided that Holt was serious, because he reached for his crutches and struggled up from the chair. "Fine," he said, "but I'm not going to be responsible when this turns out badly. You can't possibly be right, Holt. My mother is no kidnapper and certainly no master criminal with a staff. The only thing she's guilty of is falling for the wrong man who took advantage of her."

"We'll see."

ALEX FIDGETED THE ENTIRE ride to Lorraine's house. Holt and Jasper were stone silent and the tension in the car was so thick you could feel it. Lorraine's house was dark when they pulled in the drive. Holt rang the doorbell and waited, but no answer was forthcoming.

He looked back at Jasper, who hadn't bothered to get out of the car. "You've got a key, right?"

Jasper shook his head. "I am not giving you the key."

"Then I'll break the window, and you'll be party to a breaking and entering. My word and Alex's against yours. What's it going to be?"

Jasper flushed red. "You have gone too far. You're going to pay for this harassment. I'm going to see that you do."

"I'll worry about that tomorrow. The key?"

Jasper struggled with his crutches and rose from the car, completely ignoring Alex's offer of help. He dug the key out of his pocket, then limped up the sidewalk and handed it to Holt. Alex said a silent prayer that Erika was inside and alive and that Lorraine was at a long dinner at her country club or a beauty trip to New Orleans as Holt slid the key into the lock and opened the door.

"Where's the entry to the basement?" Holt asked.

"The kitchen," Jasper said, and pointed right to a hallway.

"Alex," Holt directed, "follow behind him to make sure he stays with us."

Alex nodded and fell in step behind Jasper, who shot daggers into Holt's back as he hurried down the hallway to the kitchen. The door to the basement was already open by the time Jasper and Alex reached the kitchen.

"You should get off that leg," she said, and pointed to the breakfast table.

She walked over to the basement door and looked down, but the basement took a sharp turn at the bottom of the stairs, so all she could see was the stairwell.

"Holt!" she yelled down the stairs. "Did you find anything?"

She waited a couple of seconds, but when she didn't get a response, she started to panic. What if Rommel wasn't the only criminal on Lorraine's payroll? It was something they hadn't even paused to consider, but the reality was Holt could have walked right into a trap.

"Holt!" she yelled again, then glanced back at Jasper, who was sitting at the breakfast table not even trying to mask his aggravation.

"I'm all right," Holt called out.

A wave of relief passed over her, then Holt appeared at the bottom of the stairs. When Alex saw Erika in his arms, clutching his neck and crying softly, she almost fell to the floor in relief. Holt carefully worked his way up the narrow stairwell, carrying his precious cargo as he finally stepped into the kitchen.

Jasper's jaw dropped and he stared at Erika in disbelief.

"Erika!" Alex cried, and the little girl immediately reached for her. Alex wrapped her arms around her and squeezed her tightly, not wanting to let go.

Finally, she sat the girl in a chair at the breakfast table and looked her over. "Are you hurt anywhere?"

"No," Erika said, still a little overwhelmed and weepy. "But I want Mommy."

Alex hugged her again. "Of course you do, honey. We're going to take you to Mommy in just a few minutes."

Alex looked up at Holt, who was studying Jasper.

"Do you have any idea where Lorraine is?"

Jasper shook his head, but it was clear that all the fight had gone out of him. "I don't understand…"

"She gave me a sandwich," Erika said.

"How long ago?" Alex asked.

Erika shrugged. "Not very long."

Holt opened the door to the garage and said, "Her car's still here. She may be hiding in the house."

"Where's her bedroom?" Alex asked.

"Upstairs and to the right. The first room on the left." Jasper struggled to rise from the chair and Holt helped him steady himself. He grabbed his crutches and headed for the staircase.

Alex extended her hand to Erika. "I want you to walk close behind me. Okay?"

Erika shook her head. "I don't want to see the bad woman again."

"I know, but we need to find the bad woman so the police can lock her up. That way she can't hurt you again."

Erika didn't look completely convinced, but she trusted Alex enough to believe she was safe. She put her hand in Alex's and followed her up the stairs.

As they stepped onto the landing of the second floor, Holt stepped out of the bedroom and shook his head. "She must have seen us pulling up." He picked up Erika. "The bad woman won't be able to hurt you again."

Alex sucked in a breath and stepped into the bedroom. Lorraine lay in her bed as if posed. Alex knew immediately that she was dead. Jasper was on his knees in front of the bed, sobbing softly.

"Why?" he asked. "What was the point of all this?"

Alex squeezed Jasper's shoulder as she placed her fingers on Lorraine's neck. Her body wasn't cold, but there was no sign of a pulse. An empty pill bottle stood on the nightstand, a piece of folded paper underneath it.

Even though Alex knew she should wait for

the police, she removed the letter from under the bottle and unfolded it.

Jasper,
If you're reading this, then everything went wrong, and I took the coward's way out. I want you to know that I never meant to hurt you with my actions. You are the one light in my life and I would do anything to protect you. But I could not live with your father's constant betrayals.

They were all his—the girls that disappeared years ago. While I struggled to get pregnant and suffered through miscarriages, every whore he lay down with seemed to get pregnant immediately. They all looked just like his mother when she was young. That's how I knew they were his children.

Sarah was his, too, but by the time she was born, I had you. I thought your father would change after you were born and for a long time he did. So Sarah was spared.

I couldn't believe my luck when a young, virile man like Martin showed an interest in me all those years ago. I should have known it wasn't love, but like a fool, I believed him. When I found out he was cheating on me, I couldn't handle it. It was as if I'd been transported thirty-six years into the past. Then I saw Sarah's daughter for the first time since she was a baby. She looked exactly like the other girls. I could see your father's face in hers. And I couldn't live with that.

I'm sorry I hurt you. I'm sorry I didn't choose a better father. I'll love you always,
Lorraine

SARAH WAS STANDING at the curb when Holt and Alex pulled up to her house. The car had barely stopped before Erika burst out of the backseat and ran into her mother's arms. Sarah sank to the ground, arms wrapped around her daughter, giant tears of happiness running down her cheeks.

She looked up at Alex and Holt. "Thank you."

Alex smiled at Holt, overwhelmed with relief and happiness. "It's been quite a day."

"Ha. Yeah, that's one way of putting it. At least this day had a happy ending."

"Not for Jasper."

Holt sobered. "No. I still haven't processed it all. I can't imagine what he's going to be dealing with."

"I guess we need to head to the sheriff's department and give our statements to the state police."

"We have a few minutes before they come looking for us, and I have some things I need to say to you."

"Okay." Alex felt her pulse increase, wondering what Holt was about to say.

"I was wrong. I left here believing that I couldn't be the kind of man you needed because I was destined to be just like my father and my grandfather. I never wanted you to hurt the way my mother did, and I couldn't bear the thought of having kids and having them grow up as confused as I did."

"Holt, we all make our own decisions about how we live our lives as adults. There is no part of your DNA that controls free will. You can be any man you choose to be."

"I know that now." He reached for her hand and held it gently in his. "I love you, Alex. Have always loved you. I choose to be with you…if you'll have me."

Alex choked back a cry. It was everything she'd ever wanted to hear from him and now that it was happening, she was too overwhelmed to fully comprehend it.

"I understand if you don't want a relationship," Holt continued. "I've had no good example of what a marriage should be. I've made bad decisions and run from my problems. I can only promise you that I won't run again. I may make a mess of things, but I'll stand here right in the thick of it with you."

"You fool. Of course I want you. I think I've wanted you my entire life."

She threw her arms around him and pressed her lips against his. He wrapped his arms around her and lifted her completely off the ground. Alex threw her head back and laughed, amazed at how alive she felt after all the tragedy they'd been through the past week.

Holt lowered her back to the ground and she heard Sarah clear her throat. She looked over to see her cousin and Erika grinning from ear to ear. Before she could even speak, Sarah and Erika tackled them with a bear hug. Alex and Holt each wrapped an arm around Sarah and Erika.

Family.

Chapter Eighteen

Alex hung up the phone and leaned back on the couch in Holt's cabin.

"What did your boss say?" Holt asked, as he took a seat beside her.

"She completely understood my reasons for needing a leave of absence. I want to spend some time with Sarah and Erika and make sure they're okay. I would have worked with Jasper, too, if he'd let me."

Holt sighed. "Jasper's gone. He resigned from the sheriff's position and left the state."

"I know. He came by Sarah's on his way out of town to apologize for treating her badly. We know now he'd gotten all that venom from his mother, but now that he knows the real reason for it, he's feeling pretty bad."

"What did Sarah say?"

"She cried, and hugged him, and told him everything was all right. You know Sarah."

"How's Mathilde doing?"

"She's doing well. I really appreciate you having the deputy take me out to the island today. Her hand is healing nicely and she is so tickled that we found Erika."

"And that her name is finally cleared of all wrongdoing?"

"I suppose, although she seemed to take that news with less interest. I guess she hasn't worried about what others think for so long that all it really means to her is that maybe people won't come poking around her island anymore."

Holt nodded. "Her peace has been way too long in coming."

"What about you—did you find out anything else about Rommel today when you were in New Orleans?"

"Oh, yeah. The crime scene unit lifted his prints from Lorraine's house, but they don't come up in the system. They also took some hair and ran DNA matching, and then something interesting happened. The trace came back negative in the national database, but about an hour after we ran it, the FBI called the New Orleans Police Department and started asking questions."

"Really?" Alex sat straight up on the couch. "So what do you think is going on?"

"My best guess is that whoever Rommel was

before was classified. Maybe military, maybe CIA. He must have been flying below their radar a lot of years."

"What did the FBI say?"

"Not much at all. Everything is classified, so we're not likely to get much out of them. They didn't seem all that sad to hear he was dead, though. Likely, he went rogue years ago and they've kept the feelers out but didn't want to sound an alert. From their point of view, his death is a closed file on a potential threat."

"You think he was a professional…an assassin, I mean?"

"It wouldn't surprise me."

"Wow. I guess that makes sense, but it seems so strange. I mean, why choose Vodoun?"

"I think he saw a chance to hook up with a rich, foolish woman who wouldn't ask too many questions. The feds are going over the financials at the restaurant, and he was laundering a fair amount of money through there—upwards of a million a year."

"Laundering from what?"

Holt shook his head. "Drugs, maybe. Rommel said Erika was to be sold to a Russian family. I don't like to think about the money involved in the trafficking of little girls, but it's possible some money came from that. You can bet they're trying to find it. What about you?

Did your assistance help the FBI when they searched Lorraine's home?"

"I guess. I mean, given that I knew her personally, I was able to create a better profile of her mental decline than a stranger would have."

She sighed. "We found more of the dolls in a storage bin in the basement. I can only assume she bought them years ago to implicate Mathilde and kept them. At least now we know where the dolls came from. Erika finally admitted that she'd seen the doll outside her bedroom one night and crawled out the window to get it."

"A logical explanation." He smiled. "How about that?"

"Yes, but still no logical explanation for the crows, or how Mathilde's reading was right, and definitely no logical explanation for Grand attacking Rommel."

"Are you kidding? Grand's attack on Rommel is the only thing that *does* make sense."

"Mathilde claims she's never seen Grand on that side of the island. She claims the spirits summoned him there to intercede on our behalf. That's why she threw the necklace when she did."

Holt stared at Alex. "And you believe her?"

Alex shrugged. "Why not? And besides, what does it matter why it happened when the outcome is the same. Still, I won't be so limiting with my point of view in the future. I still think there are more things unexplained in this world than explained, and a large share of them are in Mystere Parish."

"Yeah, you know, this entire situation got me to thinking."

"About what?"

"If you hadn't believed that Sarah was telling the truth and that there was no way Bobby could have taken Erika, this investigation wouldn't have happened. It was your assessment of their credibility that made me go along in the beginning, despite Jasper's objection."

"Maybe, but I think you would have gotten around to that way of thinking eventually."

"But what if it was too late once I did? Have you ever wondered how many people have been in situations like this—where they know something bad has happened, but there's no evidence for the police to go on to create a case? Meanwhile, the clock is ticking."

Alex frowned. "I guess it happens more often than I'd care to think about."

"Exactly, so I was thinking that I finally found a use for my inheritance. I want to open up a detective agency that specializes in cases where the police don't have the evidence to determine a crime has been committed."

"Oh! Holt, that's a great idea."

"And I want you to make that leave of absence permanent and be my partner."

"Me? I'm not qualified to investigate. This entire mess with Erika darn near gave me heart failure."

"I don't know. A little more training with Ms. Maude and you'd probably be chomping at the bit, but that's not what I had in mind. I was thinking you'd be perfect to assess the credibility of the clients and suspects. If you're interested, that is."

Alex stared at Holt, his idea rolling around in her mind, and the longer she thought about it, the more she liked it. After all, she'd gone into medicine to help people. This way, she'd be helping people who were out of options, but still using her medical training to do so.

"I think it sounds wonderful, and of course I want to do it." She leaned over and kissed him.

"I already have our first two cases."

"Really?"

"First, I'd like to try and find the girls who were kidnapped thirty-six years ago. Rommel said Erika was to be sold to a Russian family. If something similar happened to the other girls, we may be able to find them. It's a paper-thin chance, but I have to try."

Alex nodded. "And the second case?"

"My father's murder. Right before Grand

dragged Rommel into the bayou, his shirt sleeve came up all the way. He had the eye tattoo on his biceps. Whatever he was doing in Vodoun, Rommel wasn't doing it alone."

Alex placed her hand in Holt's and squeezed. "Let's get started."

* * * * *

Be sure to pick up the next book in Jana DeLeon's MYSTERE PARISH series when THE VANISHING goes on sale next month. Look for it wherever Harlequin Intrigue books are sold!

LARGER-PRINT BOOKS!
GET 2 FREE LARGER-PRINT NOVELS PLUS
2 FREE GIFTS!

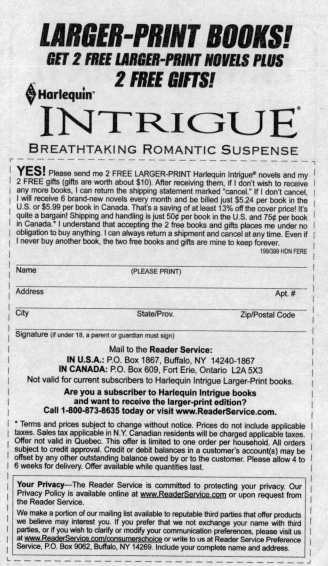

Harlequin®

INTRIGUE®

BREATHTAKING ROMANTIC SUSPENSE

YES! Please send me 2 FREE LARGER-PRINT Harlequin Intrigue® novels and my 2 FREE gifts (gifts are worth about $10). After receiving them, if I don't wish to receive any more books, I can return the shipping statement marked "cancel." If I don't cancel, I will receive 6 brand-new novels every month and be billed just $5.24 per book in the U.S. or $5.99 per book in Canada. That's a saving of at least 13% off the cover price! It's quite a bargain! Shipping and handling is just 50¢ per book in the U.S. and 75¢ per book in Canada.* I understand that accepting the 2 free books and gifts places me under no obligation to buy anything. I can always return a shipment and cancel at any time. Even if I never buy another book, the two free books and gifts are mine to keep forever.

199/399 HDN FERE

Name	(PLEASE PRINT)	
Address		Apt. #
City	State/Prov.	Zip/Postal Code

Signature (if under 18, a parent or guardian must sign)

Mail to the **Reader Service:**
IN U.S.A.: P.O. Box 1867, Buffalo, NY 14240-1867
IN CANADA: P.O. Box 609, Fort Erie, Ontario L2A 5X3
Not valid for current subscribers to Harlequin Intrigue Larger-Print books.

**Are you a subscriber to Harlequin Intrigue books
and want to receive the larger-print edition?
Call 1-800-873-8635 today or visit www.ReaderService.com.**

* Terms and prices subject to change without notice. Prices do not include applicable taxes. Sales tax applicable in N.Y. Canadian residents will be charged applicable taxes. Offer not valid in Quebec. This offer is limited to one order per household. All orders subject to credit approval. Credit or debit balances in a customer's account(s) may be offset by any other outstanding balance owed by or to the customer. Please allow 4 to 6 weeks for delivery. Offer available while quantities last.

Your Privacy—The Reader Service is committed to protecting your privacy. Our Privacy Policy is available online at www.ReaderService.com or upon request from the Reader Service.

We make a portion of our mailing list available to reputable third parties that offer products we believe may interest you. If you prefer that we not exchange your name with third parties, or if you wish to clarify or modify your communication preferences, please visit us at www.ReaderService.com/consumerschoice or write to us at Reader Service Preference Service, P.O. Box 9062, Buffalo, NY 14269. Include your complete name and address.

HILP11B

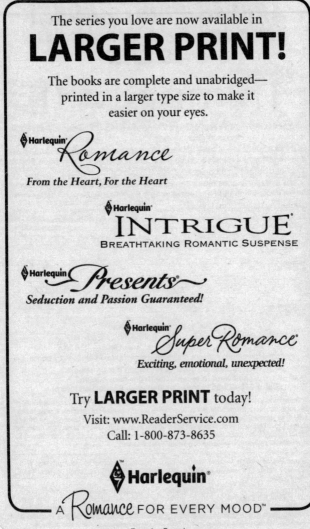